旅遊英語

—Trave— uble—

U0075118

帶 你 去 旅 行

用餐結帳 × 客房服務 × 購物血拼
見招拆招，遇到老外不再嚇到待在原地

好不容易可以出國，好想踏出平時的生活圈！
查好資料，存夠了錢，卻因為英文不好不敢向前？

學校教的英文早就忘光也別驚慌，
早就幫你整理好實用旅遊單字、短句，
吃喝玩樂，食衣住行，加上問候、標語八大主題

帶著本書一起旅行

除了必要問句，還能跟當地人閒聊，
出國旅遊想要玩得開心盡興，

就用旅遊英語360句！

張玲敏 主編

目 錄

前言

出版說明

目錄

目錄

前言

　　如今，旅遊活動在全世界都表現得異常活躍和頻繁。旅遊活動中既涉及經濟領域的交流，也涉及文化領域的交流。但不管是何種形式何種內容的交流，作為旅遊活動的主體，人與人之間的語言交流都是至關重要的。本書就是為了幫助使用不同語言的人們在旅遊活動中加強交流，提升溝通效果而編寫的。

　　本書的作者均為高級英語導遊，在旅遊業的重點單位從事接待各國賓客的工作有 20 餘年，累積了豐富的實踐經驗。尤其是主編，多年來一直是英語導遊、出國領隊等方面的職業培訓教師和考試委員，擁有豐富的相關培訓教學實踐。本書正是作者總結多年來一線工作及培訓教學經驗的基礎上編寫的。

　　本書的特點是：一切從實際出發，緊緊圍繞旅遊活動的基本環節，以場景為基本要素展開內容編寫。本書編寫思路清晰，實踐性強，且所選語句結構精練，使用頻率高。全書分為問候語、行、遊、吃、住、購、娛及其他等八個單元，各單元環環相扣，既有一定邏輯性，又相對獨立成章，方便理解和查閱。值得一提的還有本書附錄中的「實用公共標示語」部分，在實踐中具有特別的意義。

　　本書主要針對具有一定英語基礎但口語交流有困難的讀者，可以幫助他們快捷方便地進入口語交流境界。

編者

前言

出版說明

　　學習和掌握一門語言應該是一個循序漸進、不斷累積和熟練的過程，這一過程從來都不可能是一蹴而就的。學習母語之外的外語更應是這樣。本書就是基於這樣的語言學習規律編寫策劃的。同時，本書強調的語言學習理念如下：一天一句、堅持不懈，積少成多，從「量」的累積達到「質」的飛躍。

　　本書以所涉及領域的 360 個常用口語片語為特色內容，根據不同主題劃分為若干單元，每單元均設有「重點單字」和「典型對話示例」區塊，前者為學習片語「鋪路」，後者則把片語串聯成情景會話，以強化前面所學片語的適用情景，幫助學習者從操練片語向模擬情景會話過渡，逐步學會連貫地進行交談。

　　360 句的每個片語下還特別設有「關鍵句」、「應答語」、「記憶提示」和「舉一反三」四個區塊，以幫助學習者提高記憶效果，學習拓展其他的表達句式。

　　請記住並實踐我們的學習理念：一天一句、堅持不懈，積少成多，從「量」的累積達到「質」的飛躍。因為我們堅信：「只要功夫深，鐵杵磨成針」，能堅持到最後，你 ── 就是勝利者。

出版說明

Unit 1
Greetings 問候

重點單字

morning	早上（上午）
meet	遇見
China	中國
introduce	介紹
speak	講（說）
first	第一
nationality	國籍
help	幫助
nice	美好的
enjoy	享受，欣賞
come	來
all	全部的
look forward to	期待
soon	不久
glad	高興
welcome	歡迎
may	可以
myself	我自己
English	英語
visit	參觀，訪問
excuse	原諒
thank	感謝
hope	希望
stay	逗留，暫住

again	再次
best	最好的
see	看見
goodbye	再見

001　Good morning. 早安

關鍵句

A：Good morning.

A：早安（上午好）。

B：Good morning.

B：早安（上午好）。

記憶提示

此句常常是會話開頭的問候語，而對方的回答則是對於原話的複述。此句還可以簡單地說成：「Morning!」

舉一反三

（1）Good afternoon.

午安。

（2）Good evening.

晚安。

002　How do you do? 您好！

關鍵句

A：How do you do?

A：您好！

B：How do you do?

B：您好！

記憶提示

用於經人介紹初次見到某人時的問候語，所得到的回答通常仍是「How do you do?」

舉一反三

（1）Hi,Jack.

嗨，傑克。

（2）How are you?

你好嗎？

003　Glad to meet you. 很高興見到您。

關鍵句

Glad to meet you.

很高興見到您。

Glad to meet you too.

見到您我也很高興。

此句多用於第一次見面時的寒暄語，glad 在此也可用 nice，但 glad 較常用。glad 適用於一切場合，nice 則具有一定的感情色彩，有「激動、高興、愉快或盼望已久」的意思。

舉一反三

（1）Nice to meet you.
　　很高興認識您。

（2）Glad to know you.
　　很高興認識您。

004　Welcome to Taiwan. 歡迎到臺灣來。

關鍵句

Welcome to Taiwan.

歡迎到臺灣來。

Thank you.

謝謝。

記憶提示

welcome 是作為主人見到客人應該說的第一句話。根據不同場合、情景，在 to 後面加上不同的地名或事物名稱，表示歡迎的意思。

舉一反三

（1）Welcome to Taipei.
歡迎您來（到）臺北。

（2）Welcome to 2022 Olympics Winter Games.
歡迎您來 2022 年冬季奧運會。

005　May I introduce myself to you? 我可以作一下自我介紹嗎？

關鍵句

May I introduce myself to you?

我可以作一下自我介紹嗎？

Yes, please.

好，請吧。

記憶提示

introduce myself：作自我介紹。

introduce him (her, them) to sb.：向某人介紹他人。

舉一反三

（1）I'd like to introduce myself to you.
我想作個自我介紹。

（2）Please allow me to introduce myself to you.
請允許我作自我介紹。

006　Do you speak English? 你會講英語嗎？

關鍵句

Do you speak English?

您會講英語嗎？

Just a little.

會一點。

記憶提示

（1）英語中可表達為「說話」的幾個常用動詞，用法有所不同。say（說）是指用語言表述自己的思想；小孩一歲後會 speak（說話），但不能 say（述說）。tell（告訴）主要用於傳達自己的思想，talk（告訴）則著重於表示與人交談。

（2）問某人會不會講英語不要說成「Can you speak English?」因為不講英語，並不一定不會。這裡主要是遵從對方意願 —— 是否願意用英語交流，而不能按中文字面理解。

舉一反三

（1）Where did you learn your English?
你在哪裡學的英語？

（2）Shall we talk in English?
我們用英語交談怎麼樣？

007　Is this your first visit to Taipei? 這是您第一次到臺北來嗎？

關鍵句

Is this your first visit to Taipei?

這是您第一次到臺北來嗎？

Yes, exactly.

是的，沒錯。

記憶提示

first 在作形容詞或名詞時，前面要加定冠詞 the。

舉一反三

（1）Is this the first time you've been in Taipei?

這是您第一次到臺北來嗎？

（2）Was that you first trip to Taipei?

那是你第一次到臺北來嗎？

008　What's your nationality? 您是哪國人？

關鍵句

What's your nationality?

您是哪國人？

I am American.

我是美國人。

記憶提示

nationality 指國籍，常用的國籍名稱有：Taiwanese 臺灣人，Japanese 日本人，French 法國人，英國人 British。

舉一反三

（1）What nationality are you?

您是哪國人？

（2）Where are you from?
您是哪裡人（你從哪來）？

009　Excuse me. 不好意思。

關鍵句

Excuse me.

不好意思。

Yes?

什麼事？

記憶提示

「Excuse me.」作「不好意思，勞駕」時，是客氣用語，也常用於引起別人注意或請人幫忙。與人談話期間，若有突然打噴嚏、咳嗽等狀況時，此語也可用來向別人表示道歉。

舉一反三

Excuse my interruption.

請原諒，打擾了。

010　Can I help you? 需要幫忙嗎？

關鍵句

Can I help you?

需要幫忙嗎？

Yes, please.

是的。

記憶提示

這是服務行業中常用的一句話，用於客氣地詢問對方是否需要幫助。

舉一反三

（1）What can I do for you?
需要幫忙嗎？

（2）Do you need any help?
需要幫忙嗎？

011　Thank you. 謝謝。

關鍵句

Thank you.

謝謝。

You're welcome.

不客氣。

記憶提示

此句型使用率相當高，當別人為你做了事、幫了忙、送禮物時，都要說「Thank you」。特別是回答別人的讚揚時，最好的方式是欣然接受，並回以「Thank you」。

舉一反三

（1）Thanks a lot.
多謝。

（2）Thank you very much.
非常感謝。

012　You're welcome. 不客氣。

關鍵句

Thank you very much.

太感謝您了。

You're welcome.

不客氣。

記憶提示

這是回答別人感謝時的禮貌用語。

舉一反三

（1）It's my pleasure.
　　　這是我的榮幸。

（2）Not at all.
　　　不客氣。

013　Have a nice day! 祝您過得愉快！

關鍵句

Have a nice day!

祝您過得愉快！

Thanks. You too.

謝謝，也祝您愉快。

記憶提示

此句是道別時常用的祝願語。特別是朋友外出旅行，送上一句吉言，表達最美好的祝願。

舉一反三

（1）Enjoy yourself.
祝你過得快樂。

（2）Have a good stay in Taipei.
祝你在臺北過得開心。

014   Hope you enjoy your stay with us. 希望您在這裡住得愉快。

關鍵句

Hope you enjoy your stay with us.
希望您在這裡住得愉快。

Thank you very much.
非常感謝。

記憶提示

enjoy 在此是指「享受……的樂趣」；stay 停留、暫住，住在飯店用 stay in the hotel，不能用 live。live 是指長期居住。

舉一反三

（1）Hope you have a pleasant journey.
希望你們旅途愉快。

（2）Please enjoy staying with us.
希望您在此過得愉快。

015 Please come again. 歡迎再來。

關鍵句

Please come again.

歡迎再來。

I'd like to.

我會的。

記憶提示

come 與 go 的辨析：如果「來、去」的行動是說話人自己，則應以對方的位置來決定，向對方走去用 come，離開對方用 go。

舉一反三

（1）Hope you come again.
希望再見到你。

（2）Wish to see you again.
但願再見到你。

016 We look forward to seeing you soon. 期待著與您再次見面。

關鍵句

We look forward to seeing you soon.

期待著與您再次見面。

I hope so.

我也是。

記憶提示

look forward to：期待、盼望，後面接名詞或動名詞，但不能接不定式。

舉一反三

（1）Hope to meet you next time.
　　希望能與您再次見面。

（2）I really want to see you again.
　　我真希望再次見到你。

017　All the best! 祝您一切順利！

關鍵句

All the best!
祝您一切順利！
The same to you!
也祝您一切順利！

記憶提示

better 和 best 是 good 和 well 的比較級和最高級形式，best 前面一般要加 the。

舉一反三

（1）Good luck.
　　祝你好運。

（2）Best wishes to you and your family.
　　把美好的祝願送給您和您的家人。

018　Goodbye. 再見。

關鍵句

Goodbye. 再見。

Bye-bye. 再見。

記憶提示

goodbye 是正式告別用語，bye-bye 是較隨便的告別用語，see you 是常用非正式道別語。

舉一反三

（1）See you. 再見

（2）See you next time. 下次見。

Dialogue 典型對話示例

（Ⅰ）

A：Good morning. My name is Li Ping. 早安。我叫李平。

B：How do you do? I'm Jack Green. 你好，我是傑克·葛林。

A：Glad to meet you. 很高興認識你。

B：Glad to meet you. 我也很高興認識你。

A：Is this your first visit to Taipei? 這是你第一次到臺北來嗎？

B：Yes, exactly. 是的，沒錯。

A：Hope you enjoy your stay with us. 希望您在此過得愉快。

B：Thank you very much. 太感謝你了。

A：You're welcome. 不客氣。

（Ⅱ）

A：How do you do, Mr.Green? 您好，葛林先生。

B：How do you do, Miss Li? 您好，李小姐。

A：How is your trip in Taipei? 您的臺北之旅怎麼樣？

B：Very good. I enjoy it so much. 很好，我玩得非常開心。

A：Are you leaving Taipei now? 你現在就離開臺北嗎？

B：Yes. Thanks for your help. 是的。謝謝你的幫助。

A：We look forward to seeing you soon. 期待著與您再次見面。

B：I hope so. 我也是。

A：All the best! 祝您一切順利！

B：The same to you. 也祝您一切順利！

A：Goodbye. 再見。

B：Goodbye. 再見。

Unit 1 Greetings 問候

Unit 2
Traveling 旅遊

重點單字

suggest	建議
CD	光碟
several	幾個
choose from	選擇
rate	價格
pay	支付
confirm	確認
visa	簽證
vacation	假期
beach	海灘
by air	搭飛機
how often	多長時間
New York	紐約
take	占領
book	預訂
ticket	票，入場券
how about	如何
how many	多少
round trip	往返旅程
per person	每個人
included	包括的
arrival time	抵達時間
airport	機場
catch	趕上

flight number	航班號
still	還，仍然
connect	連接
prefer	寧願，更喜歡
piece	件
altogether	一共
safety belt	安全帶
suitcase	行李箱
plane	飛機
be about to land	就要著陸
right over there	就在那邊
chief means	主要方法
buy	買
Shanghai	上海
train	火車
itinerary	路線（行程）
city	城市
tour route	旅遊路線
high (peak) season	旺季
full package tour	全包式旅遊
full package tour deposit	押金
reservation	預訂
expire	期滿，終止
last week	上星期
travel	旅行
by sea	坐船

flight	航班
each week	每週
London	倫敦
economy class	經濟艙
Hangzhou	杭州
leave	離開
how much	多少錢
airport tax	機場稅
insurance	保險費
get	到達
in advance	提前
international flight	國際航班
in time	及時
window seat	靠窗口的座位
aisle seat	靠走道的座位
check-in luggage	託運行李
fasten	扣住
put	放
luggage compartment	行李艙
slow down	減速
airport shuttle bus	機場接駁巴士
railway	鐵路
transportation	運輸
soft sleeping berth	軟式臥鋪
miss	錯過
one minute	一分鐘

ship	船
maximum speed	最高速度
kilometer	公里
nowadays	現今
common phenomenon	常見現象
right turn	右轉彎
bus service	公車服務
by subway	搭地鐵
taxi	計程車
get off	下車
pass by	路過
walk	走
east	東
turn left	向左轉
break	打斷
by bicycle	騎自行車
watch out	注意
be careful	小心
easier	較容易
road	路
beware	當心
set off	起錨，開船
expressway	高速公路
per hour	每小時
traffic jam	交通堵塞
car	汽車

red light	紅燈
convenient	方便
change lines	換乘（另一條線）
bus pass	月票
round-city bus	環城巴士
Children's Park	兒童公園
bus number	車號
meter	公尺
excuse	原諒，致歉
place	地方
along the street	沿這條街
crossing	十字路口
journey	旅程
fun	有趣的事
traffic	交通
cross street	過馬路
climb up a mountain	上山
bumpy	顛簸的
bring	帶來

Section I Tour Arrangements 旅行安排

019 I'd like to suggest an itinerary for you. 我給您安排一個旅遊行程吧！

關鍵句

I'd like to suggest an itinerary for you.

我給您安排一個旅遊行程吧！

OK. Go ahead, please.

好的，請講吧！

記憶提示

suggest 這裡是「建議」，也可用 recommend。

itinerary：旅行計劃。

舉一反三

（1）I'm going to tell you the itinerary.

我來宣布一下你們的旅遊行程吧！

（2）I'd like give you some suggestion for your tour.

我給你們的旅遊行程一些建議。

020 We have several tour routes for you to choose from. 我們有幾條旅遊路線供您選擇。

關鍵句

We have several tour routes for you to choose from.

我們有幾條旅遊路線供您選擇。

Let me see, please.

請讓我看一下。

記憶提示

tour route：旅遊路線。

choose from：從……中選擇。注意：這裡的 from 不能丟掉。

舉一反三

Would you like to choose one from the tour routes I suggested to you?

你要從我提供的路線中選一條嗎？

021　It is high season rate. 這是旺季價格。

關鍵句

It is high season rate.

這是旺季價格。

OK. I also want to know the rates for other seasons.

好的。我還想知道平、淡季的價格。

記憶提示

high season = peak season：旺季

shoulder season：平季

off season：淡季

舉一反三

Rates during different seasons are not the same.

淡旺季的價格不同。

022 We have a full package tour. 我們有全包式旅遊。

關鍵句

We have a full package tour.

我們有全包式旅遊。

Very good, that's the one I'd like to book.

太好了，這正是我想預訂的。

記憶提示

a full package 指「全包式旅遊」；mini-package 指「部分包價」，即報價中只含一項或幾項服務。其他還有 individual tour，day trip 及 optional tour，分別指「自由行」、「一日遊」和「任選項目遊」。

舉一反三

（1）We have full package tours as well as mini-package and optional tours.
我們不光有全包式旅遊，還有部分包價和任選項目遊。

（2）Would like a package tour or individual tour?
您想要全包式還是自由行？

023 You need to pay a deposit. 您需要付些訂金。

關鍵句

You need to pay a deposit.

您需要付些訂金。

How much is that going to be?

要付多少？

記憶提示

deposit 是訂金，到銀行存款是 deposit money in the bank。

舉一反三

（1）You need to pay service charge.
　　您需要付服務費。

（2）You have to pay some deposit.
　　您需要付些訂金。

024　Please confirm your reservation. 請確認您的預訂。

關鍵句

Please confirm your reservation.

請確認您的預訂。

Shall I just call you?

電話預訂可以嗎？

記憶提示

confirm 是確認，對於異地購買已有座位的 OK 機票，常常需要 reconfirm（再確認）。

舉一反三

（1）I'd like to reconfirm my plane ticket.
　　我要再確認一下機票。

（2）Our hotel room has already been confirmed.
　　我們的房間已經確認好了。

025 When does your visa expire? 你的簽證什麼時候到期？

關鍵句

When does your visa expire?

你的簽證什麼時候到期？

It will be available till the end of the month.

到這個月底才到期。

記憶提示

visa：簽證

expire：到期，失效

舉一反三

（1）My visa won't be expired until next week.

我的簽證下星期到期。

（2）How long is you visa valid for?

你的簽證有效期是多長？

Section II | Traveling by Air 搭飛機旅行

026　Would you like to travel by air or by sea? 您喜歡搭飛機旅行還是坐船旅行？

關鍵句

Would you like to travel by air or by sea?

您喜歡搭飛機旅行還是坐船旅行？

By air. It saves time.

搭飛機，省時間。

記憶提示

by air：搭飛機；by sea：坐船。by：介語，在此表示交通方式。

舉一反三

（1）I prefer traveling by air.

我更喜歡搭飛機旅行。

（2）Did you go to Japan by plane or by ship last week?

上星期你是搭飛機還是坐船去日本的？

027　How often do you travel by air? 您多長時間搭飛機旅行一次？

關鍵句

How often do you travel by air?

您多長時間搭飛機旅行一次？

About once a week, I'm afraid.

恐怕一個星期坐一次。

記憶提示

how often：多久，多長。用來表示「頻率」。

舉一反三

（1）Do you travel quite often?

你經常去旅遊嗎？

（2）I do my volunteer services twice a week.

我每星期做兩次志工服務。

028 How many flights go to New York each week, please?
請問，每週有幾次到紐約的航班？

關鍵句

How many flights go to New York each week, please?

請問，每週有幾次到紐約的航班？

One flight every day except Friday.

除了星期五，每天都有一次航班。

記憶提示

each week ＝ every week：每週；a week：一週。

a flight：一個航班；a plane：一架飛機。

舉一反三

（1）We have five flights to Hong Kong every week.

我們每週有五次航班飛香港。

（2）There is a flight to Taipei every day.
每天都有一次航班飛臺北。

029　How long does it take from Taipei to London? 從臺北到倫敦要多長時間？

關鍵句

How long does it take from Taipei to London?
從臺北到倫敦要多長時間？

It's about a 16-hour flight.
大概要 16 個小時的飛行。

記憶提示

how long 在這裡表示「多長時間」。

「It takes sb. some time to do sth.」是一個固定句式，表示「做某事要占用某人多長時間」，即「某人做某事需要多長時間」。

舉一反三

（1）It will take us two hours to get to Keelung.
到基隆需要兩個小時。

（2）It's only 10 minutes to the nearest supermarket.
到最近的超市也就 10 分鐘時間。

030　I'd like two economy tickets for the 8:15 a.m. flight to Kaohsiung. 我想訂兩張上午 8 點 15 分飛高雄的經濟艙機票。

關鍵句

I'd like two economy tickets for the 8:15 a.m. flight to Kaohsiung.

我想訂兩張上午 8 點 15 分飛高雄的經濟艙機票。

No problem. We have tickets available.

沒問題,還有票。

記憶提示

economy 為 economy class 之略,指「(客機、車、船等的)經濟艙位,二等座」; business class 指「商務艙」。

舉一反三

(1) I'd like to buy a train ticket for Taichung.
  我要買一張去臺中的車票。

(2) Will you book me a plane ticket for Tokyo?
  請幫我訂一張飛東京的機票,好嗎?

031 How about the flight leaving at 7:00 a.m.? 早上 7 點起飛的航班可以嗎?

關鍵句

How about the flight leaving at 7:00 a.m.?

早上 7 點起飛的航班可以嗎?

I'm afraid it is a bit early.

恐怕有點早。

記憶提示

how about = what about:……怎麼樣?用於詢問對方意見。

舉一反三

Is the flight leaving at 7:00 a.m. OK?

早上 7 點起飛的航班可以嗎？

032　How many tickets would you like? 您要幾張票？

關鍵句

How many tickets would you like?

您要幾張票？

Two, please.

兩張。

記憶提示

how many 用於詢問數量多少，後面跟可數名詞； how much 後面跟不可數名詞。

舉一反三

How many tickets do you want?

您要幾張票？

033　How much is a round-trip ticket? 往返機票要多少錢？

關鍵句

How much is a round-trip ticket?

往返機票要多少錢？

It's US$368.

368 美元。

記憶提示

round-trip ticket：往返機票；單程票是 one-way ticket。

舉一反三

（1） How much is the one way ticket?
單程機票多少錢？

（2） What is the price for the round trip ticket?
往返機票多少錢？

034 How much is the airport tax per person? 機場稅一個人多少錢？

關鍵句

How much is the airport tax per person?
機場稅一個人多少錢？
450NT dollars.
每人 450 元。

記憶提示

airport tax：機場稅

舉一反三

（1） Do we have to pay airport tax at departure?
我們出境時要繳納機場稅嗎？

（2） How much need I pay for the airport tax?
我要繳多少機場稅？

035　Is insurance included? 保險費包含在內嗎？

關鍵句

Is insurance included?

保險費包含在內嗎？

Yes, it is.

是的，包含在內。

記憶提示

to be included 這裡是被動語態，表示「保險費包含在機票中」；如要表示「機票中包含保險費」，則用主動語態，如：The ticket includes insurance.

舉一反三

（1）Does the ticket include insurance?

機票中包含保險費嗎？

（2）Do I have to pay extra for insurance?

我還要額外付保險費嗎？

036　You'd better get to the airport two hours in advance to catch the international flight. 為趕上國際航班，您最好提前兩小時到機場。

關鍵句

You'd better get to the airport two hours in advance to catch the international flight.

為趕上國際航班，您最好提前兩小時到機場。

OK, I will.

好，我會的。

記憶提示

in advance：提前

catch 指趕上（飛機、火車、汽車），catch up with sb. 則指「追趕某人」。

舉一反三

（1） You are requested to get to the airport two hours before the flight leaves.

你得在飛機起飛前兩小時趕到機場。

（2） Please remember to be at the airport two hours in advance.

請記住，要在飛機起飛前兩小時趕到機場。

037   Could I have the flight number and arrival time? 請問您的航班號和抵達時間？

關鍵句

Could I have the flight number and arrival time?

請問您的航班號和抵達時間？

Sure, I will show you the ticket.

可以，給你看看我的機票。

記憶提示

arrival：抵達；new arrival：（商店）新（到）貨。

舉一反三

（1）Would you tell me your flight number and arrival time?
請告訴我您的航班號和抵達時間。

（2）I'd like to know your flight number and arrival time.
請告訴我您的航班號和抵達時間。

038 Am I still in time for the connecting flight? 我還來得及轉機嗎？

關鍵句

Am I still in time for the connecting flight?
我還來得及轉機嗎？

I'm afraid you have to hurry up.
恐怕您得快點了。

記憶提示

connect：連接

connecting flight：中轉聯程航班

舉一反三

（1）Do I have time for the connecting flight?
我還來得及轉機嗎？

（2）I will have the connecting flight in Hong Kong.
我要在香港轉機。

039 Can I have a window seat? 我可以要個靠窗的座位嗎？

關鍵句

Can I have a window seat?

我可以要個靠窗的座位嗎？

Let me see... OK, there it is.

讓我看一下……好的，這裡有。

記憶提示

window seat：飛機上靠窗的座位

aisle seat：靠過道的座位

舉一反三

I prefer the window seat.

我喜歡靠窗的座位。

040 I prefer an aisle seat. 我比較喜歡靠走道的座位。

關鍵句

I prefer an aisle seat.

我比較喜歡靠走道的座位。

Sorry, it's all gone.

對不起，沒有靠走道的座位了。

記憶提示

prefer：更喜歡；prefer one to another ＝ rather like one than another：兩者相比，更喜歡前者。

舉一反三

（1）I prefer an aisle seat to a window seat.
比起靠窗的座位，我更喜歡靠走道的。

（2）I'd rather like the aisle seat than the window seat.
比起靠窗的座位，我更喜歡靠走道的。

041 How many pieces of check-in luggage do you have altogether? 你們一共有多少件託運行李？

關鍵句

How many pieces of check-in luggage do you have altogether?
你們一共有多少件託運行李？

Five pieces, I think.
我想應該是五件吧。

記憶提示

check-in luggage：託運行李
luggage 為不可數名詞，要用 piece 表示件數。

舉一反三

（1）Do you have any check-in luggage?
有託運行李嗎？

（2）Please put you check-in baggage here.
請把託運行李放在這裡。

042 Do I need to fasten the safety belt? 我需要繫上安全帶嗎？

關鍵句

Do I need to fasten the safety belt?

我需要繫上安全帶嗎？

Yes, you do.

是的，一定要。

記憶提示

need to do sth.：需要做某事。

舉一反三

（1）Do I have to fasten the safety belt?

我需要繫上安全帶嗎？

（2）I need to fasten the seat belt, don't I?

我需要繫上安全帶，是嗎？

043 Would you please help me put the suitcase into the luggage compartment? 請幫我把行李箱放入行李艙內，好嗎？

關鍵句

Would you please help me put the suitcase into the luggage compartment?

請幫我把行李箱放入行李艙內，好嗎？

OK. Pass it to me, please.

好的，請把它遞給我一下。

記憶提示

help sb. (to) do sth.：在此句型中 to 可以省略。

舉一反三

（1）Could you put my suitcase into the luggage compartment?
　　請您幫我把行李箱放入行李艙內，好嗎？

（2）Would you help me with my suitcase?
　　可以請您幫我拿一下箱子嗎？

044　The plane is slowing down. We are about to land. 飛機正在減速，我們就要著陸了。

關鍵句

The plane is slowing down. We are about to land.

飛機正在減速，我們就要著陸了。

Are we going to arrive in Taipei?

我們就要到臺北了，是嗎？

記憶提示

be about to ＝ be going to：即將

舉一反三

The plane is landing now.

飛機正在降落。

045 The airport shuttle bus is right over there. 機場接駁巴士就在那邊。

關鍵句

The airport shuttle bus is right over there.

機場接駁巴士就在那邊。

Let's take the shuttle bus back to the city.

我們搭接駁巴士回市區吧！

記憶提示

shuttle bus：（接駁）班車；school shuttle bus：學校班車。

舉一反三

Where can I take the airport shuttle bus?

在哪裡可以乘坐機場接駁巴士？

Section III | About Traffic 關於交通

046 Railway is still one of the chief means of transportation in Russia. 鐵路運輸仍然是俄羅斯最主要的運輸方式之一。

關鍵句

Railway is still one of the chief means of transportation in Russia.

鐵路運輸仍然是俄羅斯最主要的運輸方式之一。

Oh, I see. Russia must have a large railway network.

噢，我知道了。俄羅斯的鐵路網一定很龐大。

記憶提示

chief means：主要方法，主要手段

舉一反三

The main transportation means in Russia is still by railway.

俄羅斯的主要運輸方式仍然是鐵路。

047　Two soft sleepers for Moscow, please. 買兩張去莫斯科的軟式臥鋪車票。

關鍵句

Two soft sleepers for Moscow, please.

買兩張去莫斯科的軟式臥鋪車票。

OK. Do you want a upper one or a lower one?

好的。要上鋪還是下鋪？

記憶提示

soft sleeper = soft-class sleeper：軟式臥鋪；hard sleeper：硬式臥鋪

舉一反三

I'd like a hard sleeper ticket for St. Petersburg.

我要買一張去聖彼得堡的硬式臥鋪票。

048 You missed the train by one minute. 您晚到了一分鐘，錯過了火車。

關鍵句

You missed the train by one minute.

您晚到了一分鐘，錯過了火車。

What lousy luck!

真倒霉！

記憶提示

miss = not catch：未趕上，錯過；失（約）；缺（勤）；缺（課）。

miss one's classes：缺課；miss school：沒有上學，缺勤。

舉一反三

（1）What a pity you didn't catch your train.

您沒趕上火車，太遺憾了。

（2）Did you fail to get on the flight?

您錯過那個航班了嗎？

049 Beware of the train, please. 請小心火車。

關鍵句

Look at the sign. We are near to the railway.

看這牌子，我們離鐵道不遠了。

Beware of the train, please.

請小心火車。

記憶提示

beware：當心，小心，一般用於祈使句中。可作為鐵路邊的警示語。

舉一反三

Look out! The train is coming.

小心！火車開過來了。

050　The ship is setting off. 船起錨了。

關鍵句

The ship is setting off.

船起錨了。

Sit tight, please.

請坐穩了。

記憶提示

set off：出發，動身。

舉一反三

（1）The ship is leaving.
　　 要開船了。

（2）The plane is going to take off soon.
　　 飛機很快就要起飛了。

051 The speed limit on Taiwan's expressways is 110 kilometers per hour. 在臺灣，高速公路最高限速為每小時 110 公里。

關鍵句

The speed limit on Taiwan 's expressways is 110 kilometers per hour.

在臺灣，高速公路最高限速為每小時 110 公里。

It's about the same as our country.

和我們國家差不多。

記憶提示

maximum ＝ most：最高的，最大的。

speed 這裡指 speed limit（限速）。

舉一反三

What is the speed limit for streets in downtown area?

市區街道限速是多少？

052 Nowadays a traffic jam is a common phenomenon in big cities of USA. 如今，塞車在美國的大城市是常見現象。

關鍵句

Nowadays a traffic jam is a common phenomenon in big cities of USA.

如今，塞車在美國的大城市是常見現象。

I think it's the same problem in big cities all over the world.

我想這是世界各大城市都存在的問題。

57

記憶提示

traffic jam：交通堵塞。

common ＝ normal：普遍的，平常的。

common phenomenon：普遍現象。

舉一反三

（1）We always have heavy traffic in large cities in USA.
美國大城市的交通總是很擁塞。

（2）Cars move so slowly during the rush hour.
上下班高峰時，車子行駛很緩慢。

> 053　In some countries, the car can still make a right turn when the red light is on. 在某些國家，紅燈亮時汽車仍能右轉彎。

關鍵句

In some countries, the car can still make a right turn when the red light is on.

在某些國家，紅燈亮時汽車仍能右轉彎。

But it's forbidden in most cities in our country.

但在我們國家的多數城市是不允許的。

記憶提示

make a right turn ＝ turn right：右轉彎；左轉彎是 left turn。

舉一反三

（1）The right turn is allowed when the red light is on.

當紅燈亮時，汽車允許右轉彎。

（2）There is no left turn on this street.

這條路不能左轉彎。

---

054 Please watch out for the traffic while crossing the street. 過馬路時，請注意來往車輛。

關鍵句

Please watch out for the traffic while crossing the street.

過馬路時，請注意來往車輛。

Thanks for reminding us.

謝謝你提醒。

記憶提示

watch out (for) = look out：小心、注意。

舉一反三

Be careful when crossing streets.

過馬路時要小心。

---

055 The road is bumpy. 路上很顛簸。

關鍵句

The road is bumpy.

路上很顛簸。

Yes, it needs repairs.

是的，這路該修了。

記憶提示

bumpy：顛簸的；bumpy road：顛簸的路。

舉一反三

（1）We are driving along the bumpy road.

我們行駛在崎嶇的路上。

（2）The road is rather rough.

這條路太顛簸了。

Section IV　Asking for Directions 問路

056　Bus service is convenient in Taipei. 臺北的公車服務系統很方便。

關鍵句

Bus service is convenient in Taipei.

臺北的公車服務系統很方便。

There must be many people going to work by bus.

一定有很多人坐公車上下班。

記憶提示

convenient：方便的

convenience 是 convenient 的名詞形式。

for convenience：為方便起見。

舉一反三

（1） It's very convenient to take a bus.
搭公車很方便。

（2） It's quite fast to get there by subway.
搭地鐵到那裡很快捷的。

---

057 Do I have to buy another ticket when I change lines?
換乘另一條線時還要再買票嗎？

關鍵句

Do I have to buy another ticket when I change lines?
換乘另一條線時還要再買票嗎？

No, you don't.
不需要。

記憶提示

change lines 這裡指「換乘地鐵另一條路線」；change a bus 指「換乘公車」。

舉一反三

（1） Do I need another ticket when I change lines?
換乘另一條線時還要再買票嗎？

（2） Should I buy another ticket for changing lines?
換乘另一條線時還要再買票嗎？

058　Would you like me to call a taxi for you? 需要我幫您叫輛計程車嗎？

關鍵句

Would you like me to call a taxi for you?

需要我幫您叫輛計程車嗎？

I will be glad if you do so.

你能幫忙我很高興。

記憶提示

call a taxi 在此也可以說 get a taxi。

舉一反三

（1）Do you want a taxi now?

你現在需要計程車嗎？

（2）I'd like to get a taxi for you.

我為您叫輛計程車吧。

059　Would you please show me your ticket or bus pass when you get off? 下車時請出示您的車票或月票。

關鍵句

Would you please show me your ticket or bus pass when you get off?

下車時請出示您的車票或月票。

Yes, here is my ticket.

好，這是我的票。

記憶提示

show：出示；show 和不同介詞搭配能表示不同意思，如 show off（炫耀），show up（出席、露面）等。

舉一反三

（1）Please let me see your ticket or bus pass when you get off.
下車時請出示您的車票或月票。

（2）Please get your ticket or bus pass ready when you get off.
下車時請出示您的車票或月票。

060　You can go there by subway. 您可以搭地鐵去。

關鍵句

How do I get to the railway station?
我搭什麼車去火車站？
You can go there by subway.
您可以搭地鐵去。

記憶提示

subway：地鐵，是美式英語用法，英式英語用 underground。

舉一反三

（1）You can take subway to get there.
您可以搭地鐵去。

（2）It's faster to go by underground.
搭地鐵去快一些。

061　How often do the buses come? 多久來一班公車？

關鍵句

How often do the buses come?

多長時間來一班公車？

They come every five to ten minutes.

5 ～ 10 分鐘一班。

記憶提示

how often：多久一次。

舉一反三

How often do the buses run?

多長時間來一班車？

062　Is it a round-city bus? 這是環城公車嗎？

關鍵句

Is it a round-city bus?

這是環城公車嗎？

Sorry, I'm not sure.

抱歉，我不太清楚。

記憶提示

round-city：環城的；環路是 ring road。

舉一反三

（1）Is the bus going around the city?

這是環城公車嗎？

（2）Bus No.300 goes along the Roosevelt Road.

300 號公車沿羅斯福路行駛。

063　It will take you only 15 minutes. 15 分鐘就可以到達。

關鍵句

How long does it take to get there?

到那裡需要多長時間？

It will take you only 15 minutes.

15 分鐘就可以到達。

記憶提示

take：花費，需要。

舉一反三

（1）It's only 15-minute ride.

只要 15 分鐘車程即可到達。

（2）Can I get there in 15 minutes?

15 分鐘能到達嗎？

064　Does this bus pass by the Children's Park? 這輛公車經過兒童公園嗎？

關鍵句

Does this bus pass by the Children's Park?

這輛公車經過兒童公園嗎？

Yes, it's the right one.

對，正是這臺車。

記憶提示

pass by：路過，經過。

舉一反三

（1）Can I take this bus to the Children's Park?

搭這輛公車能到兒童公園嗎？

（2）Can I go to the Children's Park by this bus?

搭這輛公車能到兒童公園嗎？

065　Could you tell me which bus I need to take? 請問我需要搭乘哪號公車？

關鍵句

I'd like to go to the 228 Peace Park. Could you tell me which bus do I need to take?

我想去二二八和平公園，請問我需要搭乘哪一號公車？

Bus No.101 can take you to the front gate of Beihai Park.

101 號公車路過北海前門。

記憶提示

need 在此不是情態動詞，在隨後的動詞前要加 to。

舉一反三

（1）Which bus is for the 228 Peace Park?
搭哪一號公車能到二二八和平公園？

（2）Which bus shall I take to the 228 Peace Park?
搭哪一號公車能到二二八和平公園？

066 First take Bus No.1 to National Taiwan University Hospital, then walk 100 meters east and you'll get there.
先搭 1 號車到臺大醫院，再朝東走 100 公尺就到了。

關鍵句

First take Bus No.1 to National Taiwan University Hospital, then walk 100 meters east and you'll get there.

先搭 1 號公車到臺大醫院，再朝東走 100 公尺就到了。

Oh, I see. Thank you.

謝謝，我明白了。

記憶提示

go east：向東走

go west：向西走

舉一反三

Take the subway and get off at National Taiwan University Hospital station.

搭地鐵到臺大醫院站下車。

067　May I ask where I am and how can I get to the Huashan Spot Theater? 請問，這裡是什麼地方，我要去光點華山電影館該怎麼走？

關鍵句

May I ask where I am and how can I get to the Huashan Spot Theater?
請問，這裡是什麼地方，我要去光點華山電影館該怎麼走？

It's Syntrend Creative Park. Go up this road about 200 meters, then you can see the Theater.
這裡是三創生活園區，沿這條路向前走 200 公尺就可以看到戲院大樓了。

舉一反三

Is the Huashan Spot Theater within walking distance?
可以從這裡走著去光點華山電影館嗎？

068　Go along the street and turn left at the crossing. 沿這條街向前走，十字路口處向左轉。

關鍵句

Go along the street and turn left at the crossing.
沿這條街向前走，十字路口處向左轉。

Is that still far from here?
離這裡很遠嗎？

記憶提示

go along：沿著；go up（down）：向北（南）走。

舉一反三

（1）Go down the road and turn right at the first crossing.
沿這條路向南，第一個路口右轉。

（2）Go straight ahead about 150 meters.
直著往前走大概 150 公尺就是了。

069　I can show you there. 我可以帶您去那裡。

關鍵句

I can show you there.
我可以帶您去那裡。

It's very kind of you.
您真是太好了。

記憶提示

take 這裡是帶領的意思，take 和不同的介詞或副詞搭配有不同的意思，如 take away 拿走，take over 接收，take up 著手處理。

舉一反三

Let me show you there.
讓我領您過去吧！

070　Can I break the journey? 我可以中途下車嗎？

關鍵句

Can I break the journey?
我可以中途下車嗎？

Sorry, you can't.

抱歉，不可以。

記憶提示

break the journey：中斷旅程。

舉一反三

（1）Can I get off the bus wherever I want?

我想在哪裡下車都行嗎？

（2）May I get off between two bus stops?

我可以在兩站之間下車嗎？

071　Traveling by bicycle is fun. 騎自行車旅行很有趣。

關鍵句

Traveling by bicycle is fun.

騎自行車旅行很有趣。

I think so, too.

我也這樣認為。

舉一反三

（1）It's fun to travel by bicycle.

騎自行車旅行很有趣。

（2）I like traveling by bicycle.

我喜歡騎自行車旅行。

072 Do you have bicycles for rent? 你們有自行車出租嗎？

關鍵句

Do you have bicycles for rent?

你們有自行車出租嗎？

Yes, we do.

是的，有。

記憶提示

（1）for rent：供出租。

（2）有的旅遊景點有出租輪椅（wheel chair）、嬰兒車（baby carriage）、語音導遊機（audio guide）的服務。

舉一反三

Any bicycles available for rent?

有自行車出租嗎？

073 The rent is 600 NT dollars a day. 租金 600 元一天。

關鍵句

How much is the rent for a day?

一天的租金是多少？

The rent is 600 NT dollars a day.

租金 600 元一天。

記憶提示

（1）per：每。

例：Twenty NT dollars per copy. 每冊二十元。

（2）percent：百分之……

例：About 35 percent of the drivers are female.

大約 35% 的司機是女性。

舉一反三

The rent is 600 NT dollars each day.

租金 600 元一天。

Dialogue 典型對話示例

（Ⅰ）

A：Hello, can I help you?

您好，我能幫忙嗎？

B：I'd like to book a trip to Japan.

我想預訂去日本的旅遊行程。

A：We have several tour routes for you to choose from.

我們這有幾條路線供你選擇。

B：It's very nice.

太好了。

（Ⅱ）

A：I'd like to book two tickets for Tokyo.

我要訂兩張飛東京的機票。

B：How about the flight leaving at 7:00 a.m.?

7 點起飛的航班可以嗎？

A：It's all right. How much?

可以。多少錢？

B：8,900 NT dollars each.

每張 8,900 元。

A：Is insurance included?

保險費包含在內嗎？

B：Yes, it is. Please remember you'd better get to the airport two hours in advance.

是的，包含保險費。請記得最好提前兩小時到機場。

A：OK, I will.

好的，我會的。

（Ⅲ）

A：I'd like to go to the 228 Peace Park. Could you tell me which bus I need to take?

我想去二二八和平公園，請問我要搭幾號公車？

B：Bus No.101 passes by the front gate of 228 Peace Park.

101 號公車車路過二二八和平公園前門。

A：How often do the buses come?

多長時間一班車？

B：They come every five to ten minutes.

5 ～ 10 分鐘一班。

（Ⅳ）

A：May I ask where I am and how can I get to the Huashan Spot Theater?

請問，這裡是什麼地方，光點華山電影館怎麼走？

B：It's Syntrend Creative Park. Go up this road about 200 meters, then you can see the theater.

這裡是三創生活園區，沿這條路往前走 200 公尺就可以看到戲院了。

I can show you there.

我可以帶你去那裡。

A：It's very kind of you.

您真是太好了。

B：Please watch out for the traffic while crossing the streets.

過馬路時，請注意來往車輛。

A：Thanks for reminding me.

謝謝您的提醒。

Unit 2   Traveling 旅遊

Unit 3
Sightseeing 觀光

重點單字

abroad	海外
become	成為
trendy	新潮的，流行的
terra-cotta horses and warriors	兵馬俑
consider	認為
garden	花園
unique	唯一的，獨特的
under heaven	天下
renowned	有名的
Buddhist	佛教的
major	主要的
scenic spot	景點
landscape	風景，山水畫
list	名錄
human	人類
natural	自然的
cultural heritage	文化遺產
UNESCO	聯合國教科文組織
mural	壁畫
grotto	窟，洞穴
make up	構成
important part	重要部分
world	世界
culture	文化

capital	首都
million	百萬
history	歷史
continental climate	大陸性氣候
foreign tourist	外國遊客
beautiful	美麗的
historical interests	古蹟
must	必須
famous	著名的
symbol	象徵
unfortunately	不幸地
destroy	毀壞
invader	入侵者
emperor	皇帝
worship	祭祀
Ming and Qing dynasties	明清兩代
heaven	天
pray	祈禱
good harvest	豐收
magnificent	宏偉的
temple	寺廟
Lamaism	喇嘛教
giant panda	大熊貓
national treasure	國寶
karst cave	石灰岩（喀斯特）溶洞
skull	頭蓋骨

excavate	挖掘
ideal	理想的
red leaves	紅葉
fall	秋天
during	在……期間
heart	心
ache	疼痛
cable car	纜車
remember	記住
park	停車
until	到……為止
minute	分鐘
take pictures/photos	照相
hold on	拿著
admission ticket	門票
later	稍後，以後
inside	裡面
building	建築物（大樓）
side entrance	旁門
family	家庭
wait for	等待
follow	跟著
arrow	箭頭
restroom	洗手間
dead end	死胡同
bottled water	瓶裝水

film	底片
booth	售貨亭
suntan	曬黑
eye	眼睛
kid	小孩子
too young	太年輕
climb	爬
household	家庭
Palace Museum	故宮博物院

Section I About Famous Sights 名勝

074 Terra-cotta horses and warriors in Xi'an are considered as the eighth wonder of the world. 西安兵馬俑被認為是世界第八大奇蹟。

關鍵句

Terra-cotta horses and warriors in Xi'an are considered as the eighth wonder of the world.

西安兵馬俑被認為是世界第八大奇蹟。

I think it is absolutely right.

我認為絕對是。

記憶提示

terra-cotta horses and warriors：兵馬俑。

wonder of the world：世界奇蹟。

舉一反三

Terra-cotta horses and soldiers in Xi'an are as famous as the seven wonders of the world.

西安兵馬俑和世界七大奇蹟同樣著名。

075　Lin Family Mansion and Garden is unique under heaven. 林本源園邸舉世無雙。

關鍵句

Lin Family Mansion and Garden is unique under heaven.

林本源園邸舉世無雙。

Really, I won't miss it.

真的，我絕不能錯過。

記憶提示

unique = only one：獨一無二的，唯一的。

舉一反三

（1）Lin Family Mansion and Garden is famous for its unique gardens.
林本源園邸以其獨特的園林而著稱。

（2）Lin Family Mansion and Garden is very pretty.
林本源園邸的園林非常漂亮。

076 Jade Mountain is one of the renowned mountains in Taiwan. 玉山是臺灣的名山之一。

關鍵句

Jade Mountain is one of the renowned mountains in Taiwan.

玉山是臺灣的名山之一。

記憶提示

renowned ＝ well-known ＝ famous：有名的。

舉一反三

（1）Jade Mountain is one of the four famous Mountains in Taiwan.

玉山是臺灣的名山之一。

（2）Jade Mountain has lovely scenery.

玉山風景秀麗。

077 Yuguang Island is one of the major scenic spots in Tainan. 漁光島是臺南的主要景點之一。

關鍵句

Yuguang Island is one of the major scenic spots in Tainan.

漁光島是臺南的主要景點之一。

It's one of my favorite places in Taiwan.

那是我最喜歡的臺灣景點之一。

記憶提示

scenic spot：景點；place of interest：名勝。

舉一反三

Yuguang Island is one of the most beautiful places in Taiwan.

漁光島是臺灣景色最優美的地方之一。

078   Guilin's landscape is second to none. 桂林山水甲天下。

關鍵句

Guilin's landscape is second to none.

桂林山水甲天下。

I must go there when I have a chance.

我有機會一定會去的。

記憶提示

second to none：首屈一指的。也可說 second to no one。

舉一反三

（1）Hualien is well-known for its graceful hills and clear water.
花蓮以山清水秀而聞名遐邇。

（2）Taroko is one of the famous scenic spots in Hualien.
太魯閣是花蓮的一個著名景點。

079   Itsukushima-jinja Shrine has been included in the UN-ESCO world heritage list. 嚴島神社已被聯合國教科文組織列入世界遺產名錄。

關鍵句

Itsukushima-jinja Shrine has been included in the UNESCO world heritage list.

嚴島神社已被聯合國教科文組織列入世界遺產名錄。

Itsukushima-jinja Shrine is well worth the honor.

嚴島神社獲得這個榮譽是應該的。

記憶提示

UNESCO（United Nations Educational, Scientific and Cultural Organization）是「聯合國教科文組織」的英文名稱的縮寫。

舉一反三

（1）Itsukushima-jinja Shrine has been enlisted in the world heritage by UNESCO.

嚴島神社已被聯合國教科文組織列入世界遺產名錄。

（2）Itsukushima-jinja Shrine is one of the world heritages. 嚴島神社是世界遺產之一。

---

080 Murals in Dunhuang Grottoes make up an important part of the world Buddhist culture. 敦煌壁畫是世界佛教文化的重要組成部分。

關鍵句

Murals in Dunhuang Grottoes make up an important part of the world Buddhist culture.

敦煌壁畫是世界佛教文化的重要組成部分。

I'm eager to see them with my own eyes.

我太想去親眼看看了。

記憶提示

make up of sth.：由什麼組成。

Buddhist （佛教的）是 Buddhism （佛教）的形容詞形式。

舉一反三

Murals in Dunhuang Grottoes take an important role in the world Buddhist culture.

敦煌壁畫是世界佛教文化的重要組成部分。

081　The beach in Kenting, is one of the best in Taiwan. 墾丁的海灘是臺灣最好的海灘之一。

關鍵句

The beach in Kenting, is one of the best in Taiwan.

墾丁的海灘是臺灣最好的海灘之一。

I'd like to make a trip there next year.

我準備明年去那裡一趟。

記憶提示

best 是 good 的最高級，best 前面一定要加定冠詞 the。

舉一反三

The best beach in Taiwan can be seen in Kenting.

在墾丁可以看到臺灣最好的海灘。

Section II | Sightseeing 觀光

082　Taipei is the capital of Taiwan. 臺北是臺灣的首都。

關鍵句

Taipei is the capital of Taiwan.

臺北是臺灣的首都。

How long has it been the capital for Taiwan?

臺北作為臺灣的首都有多久了？

記憶提示

the capital of a country 是國家的首都。

舉一反三

（1）Beijing was the capital of Jin, Yuan, Ming, Qing dynasties for over 800 years.

北京作為金、元、明、清四朝古都有 800 多年的歷史。

（2）The capital of Taiwan is Taipei.

臺灣的首都是臺北。

083　Tokyo is a big city with over 13 million people. 東京是一個有 1,300 多萬人口的大城市。

關鍵句

Tokyo is a big city with over 13 million people.

東京是一個有 1,300 多萬人口的大城市。

My God! So many people in Tokyo!

我的天！東京有那麼多人口！

記憶提示

over ＝ more than：多於，超過。

舉一反三

（1）Tokyo is a large city with a population of over 13 million.

東京有 1,300 多萬人口。

（2）Osaka is the third largest city of Japan in terms of population.

大阪是日本第三大人口最多的城市。

084　Kyoto has a history of over 1,000 years. 京都有一千多年的歷史。

關鍵句

Kyoto has a history of over 1,000 years.

京都有一千多年的歷史。

Oh, it has such a long history.

哦，京都的歷史真長。

記憶提示

history：歷史。此詞可分解為「hi (s) ＋ story」（他的故事）來記憶。

舉一反三

（1）Kyoto is an ancient city with a history of over 1,000 years.

京都是一座有千年歷史的古城。

（2）The history of Kyoto dated back to 1,000 years ago.
京都的歷史可追溯到 1,000 年前。

085 USA has a continental climate. 美國屬大陸性氣候。

關鍵句

USA has a continental climate.

美國屬大陸性氣候。

I guess it's not bad.

我想氣候還不錯吧。

記憶提示

continental：大陸的；其名詞形式為 continent（大陸）。

climate 是氣候，而 weather 是天氣，不能混用。

舉一反三

（1）The climate in Japan is with four distinct seasons.
日本的氣候四季分明。

（2）The climate in Tokyo is not bad except for dryness.
東京的氣候還不錯，就是乾燥。

086 This is the best time to visit Tokyo. 現在正是遊覽東京的最好時候。

關鍵句

This is the best time to visit Tokyo.

現在正是遊覽東京的最好時候。

Then we have made a wise choice to come now.

看來我們選擇現在來是明智的。

記憶提示

best time：最好的時候。

舉一反三

（1）The best time to visit Kyoto is spring and autumn.

春秋季節是遊覽京都的最好時候。

（2）I suggest you come to Kyoto in September and October.

我建議你們最好在九月、十月時來京都。

087　Kyoto is a beautiful city with a lot of scenic spots and places of historical interest. 京都是個有著許多風景名勝和歷史古蹟的城市。

關鍵句

Kyoto is a beautiful city with a lot of scenic spots and places of historical interest.

京都是個有著許多風景名勝和歷史古蹟的城市。

So I need longer time to stay in Kyoto.

所以我要在京都多待些時間。

記憶提示

a lot of：許多，後面可以接可數名詞和不可數名詞。

舉一反三

（1）Kyoto is a famous city with rich history and culture.

京都是具有豐富歷史文化的名城。

（2）Kyoto has many scenic spots and places of historical interest.
京都有著許多風景名勝和歷史古蹟。

088　Kiyomizu Temple is a must. 清水寺一定要去。

關鍵句

Kiyomizu Temple is a must.

清水寺一定要去。

It has been my dream to go to Kiyomizu Temple.

去看看清水寺一直是我的夢想。

記憶提示

must 這裡是名詞，意為「必須要做的事」。

舉一反三

（1）It's a great pity if you come to Kyoto without touring Kiyomizu Temple.
如果到京都不去清水寺，那就太遺憾了。

（2）Touring Kiyomizu Temple should be the first choice while touring Kyoto.
到京都旅遊時的第一選擇應該是去清水寺。

089　Times Square is the biggest city central square in the world. 時報廣場是世界上最大的城市中心廣場。

關鍵句

Times Square is the biggest city central square in the world.

時報廣場是世界上最大的城市中心廣場。

I didn't realize it is so large.

我真沒想到它有這麼大。

記憶提示

biggest 是 big 的最高級，前面要加 the。

舉一反三

Dadaocheng is very famous for many historical events which happened there.

大稻埕由於發生過許多歷史事件而聞名。

090　The Palace Museum is worth seeing. 故宮很值得一看。

關鍵句

The Palace Museum is worth seeing.

故宮很值得一看。

OK, we are not going to miss it.

好的，我們不會錯過的。

記憶提示

be worth sth. 是「值得……」的意思，be worth doing sth. 是「值得做某事」。例如：

The place is worth a visit.

這地方值得一去。

That makes life worth living.

那樣才活得有意義。

舉一反三

（1）The Palace Museum is one of the must-sees for tourists in Taiwan.

對來臺灣的旅遊者來說，故宮是必看景點之一。

（2）Palacio Real is the best preserved imperial palace in the world.

馬德里王宮是世界上保存最完好的皇家宮殿。

091 The Summer Palace is famous for its beautiful scenery. 頤和園以風景美麗著稱。

關鍵句

The Summer Palace is famous for its beautiful scenery.

頤和園以風景美麗著稱。

I must take more pictures there.

我一定要在那裡多拍些照片。

記憶提示

scenery ＝ landscape：景色、風景。

舉一反三

The Summer Palace has beautiful scenery with a hill and a lake.

頤和園有山有水，風景秀麗。

092　The Tower of Buddhist Incense is the symbol of the Summer Palace. 佛香閣是頤和園的象徵。

關鍵句

The Tower of Buddhist Incense is the symbol of the Summer Palace.

佛香閣是頤和園的象徵。

What a splendid building!

多麼輝煌的建築啊！

記憶提示

symbol：標誌，象徵。

舉一反三

（1）The Tower of Buddhist Incense is the highest point of the Summer Palace.

佛香閣是頤和園的最高點。

（2）The Tower of Buddhist Incense is a unique structure.

佛香閣是一個獨特的建築。

093　Yuanmingyuan, once a garden of gardens, unfortunately was destroyed by foreign invaders. 曾是萬園之園的圓明園不幸被外國入侵者毀壞了。

關鍵句

Yuanmingyuan, once a garden of gardens, unfortunately was destroyed by foreign invaders.

曾是萬園之園的圓明園不幸被外國入侵者毀壞了。

What a pity!

太可惜了。

記憶提示

unfortunately：不幸地、令人遺憾地。

destroy ＝ damage ＝ ruin：破壞、毀壞。

舉一反三

（1）Yuanmingyuan, once a beautiful garden, was damaged by foreign invaders.

曾經美麗的圓明園被外國入侵者毀壞了。

（2）The imperialist powers burnt down Yuanmingyuan in 1860.

外國列強在 1860 年燒毀了圓明園。

---

094 The Temple of Heaven is the place where the emperors of the Ming and Qing dynasties worshiped heaven and prayed for good harvest. 天壇是明清兩代皇帝祭天祈禱豐收的地方。

關鍵句

The Temple of Heaven is the place where the emperors of the Ming and Qing dynasties worshiped heaven and prayed for good harvest.

天壇是明清兩代皇帝祭天祈禱豐收的地方。

I guess it was a very important place for emperors.

我想，對皇帝來說，那一定是非常重要的地方。

記憶提示

worship：祭拜、做禮拜；pray：祈禱、祈求。

舉一反三

（1）The Temple of Heaven is the place for emperors of the Ming and Qing dynasties to worship heaven and pray for good harvest.

天壇是明清兩代皇帝祭天祈禱豐收的地方。

（2）The emperors would come to the Temple of Heaven for worshiping the heaven and praying for good harvest.

皇帝到天壇去祭天並祈禱五穀豐登。

095   Yonghe Palace is the biggest lama temple in Beijing.
雍和宮是北京最大的一座喇嘛廟。

關鍵句

Yonghe Palace is the biggest lama temple in Beijing.

雍和宮是北京最大的一座喇嘛廟。

I'm very interested in Lamaism.

我對喇嘛教很感興趣。

記憶提示

Yonghe Palace：雍和宮，也稱 Lama Temple （喇嘛廟）。

magnificent 可用來形容建築的宏偉，也可用來形容天氣好，如：

magnificent weather （極好的天氣）。

舉一反三

（1）Yonghe Palace, also known as lama Temple, is an imperial temple of Lamaism.

雍和宮又稱喇嘛廟，是一座皇家喇嘛教寺廟。

（2）Lama Temple is one of the best preserved complexes of ancient architecture.

喇嘛廟是保存最完好的古建築群之一。

---

096 The Lone Pine Koala Sanctuary is the best place to see a koala, the national treasure of Australia. 龍柏動物園是觀賞澳洲國寶無尾熊的最佳去處。

關鍵句

The Lone Pine Koala Sanctuary is the best place to see a koala, the national treasure of Australia.

龍柏動物園是觀賞澳洲國寶無尾熊的最佳去處。

Koalas are so cute.

無尾熊太可愛了。

記憶提示

treasure：珍寶。

舉一反三

（1）The best place to visit a koala is the Lone Pine Koala Sanctuary.

龍柏動物園是觀賞澳洲國寶無尾熊的最佳去處。

（2）Let's go to the Zoo to see a koala.

我們去動物園看無尾熊吧！

---

097 Gorilla Cave is a nice karst cave in Kaohsiung. 高雄猩猩洞是一個漂亮的石灰岩溶洞。

關鍵句

Gorilla Cave is a nice karst cave in Kaohsiung.

高雄猩猩洞是一個漂亮的石灰岩溶洞。

Is there anything interesting?

那裡有什麼有趣的東西嗎？

記憶提示

cave：洞穴；karst：石灰岩，喀斯特地貌。

舉一反三

（1）Gorilla Cave is a marvelous karst cave.

猩猩洞是個奇特的石灰岩溶洞。

（2）There is a karst cave in Kaohsiung called Gorilla Cave.

高雄有一個石灰岩溶洞叫猩猩洞。

098　Neander Valley is the place where　Neanderthals' remains was first excavated in 1856. 尼安德河谷是 1856 年首次挖掘出尼安德塔人遺跡的地方。

關鍵句

Neander Valley is the place where Neanderthals' remains was first excavated in 1856.

尼安德河谷是 1856 年首次挖掘出尼安德塔人遺跡的地方。

Can we see the remains in the museum?

我們在博物館能見到那些遺跡嗎？

記憶提示

excavate：挖掘、發掘。

舉一反三

Neanderthals' remains was first excavated in Neander Valley in 1856.

1856 年在尼安德河谷第一次挖掘出尼安德塔人遺跡。

099 Aowanda is an ideal place to enjoy red leaves in the fall. 奧萬大國家森林遊樂區是秋天觀賞紅葉的好去處。

關鍵句

Aowanda is an ideal place to enjoy red leaves in the fall.

奧萬大國家森林遊樂區是秋天觀賞紅葉的好去處。

So, is there not much to see in spring and summer?

那麼，春天和夏天就沒什麼可看的了？

記憶提示

ideal：理想的；fall〈主美〉＝ autumn〈主英〉：秋天。

舉一反三

（1）We can enjoy red leaves in the Aowanda in autumn.

秋天，我們可以去奧萬大國家森林遊樂區觀賞紅葉。

（2）Many people like climbing the Dakeng every day.

許多人喜歡每天去爬大坑。

100　It's easier to climb up a mountain than down. 上山容易下山難。

關鍵句

It's easier to climb up a mountain than down.

上山容易下山難。

I guess it is indeed.

我想的確是這樣。

記憶提示

easier 是 easy 的比較級；than down 是 than to go down 的簡略形式。

舉一反三

（1）Climbing up a mountain is easier than going down.

上山容易下山難。

（2）It's harder to go down a mountain than up.

上山容易下山難。

101　My heart aches for a visit already. 我已經迫不及待地想去參觀了。

關鍵句

My heart aches for a visit already.

我已經迫不及待地想去參觀了。

OK, let's go immediately.

好吧，馬上走。

記憶提示

ache：痛，通常可作為後綴放在名詞後面，表示哪裡痛。如：head-ache，toothache 等。但在本句中 ache 是動詞，表示「渴望」。

舉一反三

（1）I can hardly wait.
我已經迫不及待了。

（2）I'm eager to go right now.
我真想立刻就走。

---

102 We are going to stay here for about 2 hours. 我們會在這裡待大約兩個小時。

關鍵句

We are going to stay here for about 2 hours.
我們會在這裡待大約兩個小時。

That's great!
太好了！

記憶提示

stay for 後接時間短語，表示停留時間的長度。

舉一反三

（1）We are going to spend two hours here.
我們會在這裡待兩個小時。

（2）I think two hours will be enough in the museum.
我想用兩個小時參觀博物館足夠了。

103   We'll have 10 minutes to take pictures. 給大家十分鐘照相時間。

關鍵句

We'll have 10 minutes to take pictures.

給大家十分鐘照相時間。

That's a good idea.

太好了。

記憶提示

take a picture = take a photo：拍照；如請別人給自己拍照要用「have one's photo taken」。

舉一反三

（1）I'll leave you 10 minutes for taking pictures.

給大家十分鐘照相時間。

（2）There are 10 minutes for you to take photos.

給大家十分鐘照相時間。

104   Please hold on to the admission tickets, you will need it later inside. 請拿好門票，到裡面還要用。

關鍵句

Please hold on to the admission tickets, you will need it later inside.

請拿好門票，到裡面還要用。

I'll keep it as a souvenir anyway.

反正我也要把它當紀念品收藏的（我不會扔掉的）。

記憶提示

admission ticket：入場券、門票；admission free：免費入場。

hold on to：拿好、抓住。

舉一反三

（1）Keep your admission tickets, you still need it inside.
門票別丟了，到裡面還要用。

（2）Do not throw away the admission tickets until you finish the visit here.
參觀完之前不要把門票扔了。

105 This building was first built in the Ming Dynasty. 此建築始建於明朝。

關鍵句

This building was first built in the Ming Dynasty.
此建築始建於明朝。

It still looks perfect.
看起來還是那麼完好。

記憶提示

first build：始建於； rebuild：重建。

舉一反三

This is a hall first built in the Ming Dynasty.
此大殿始建於明朝。

106　Mr.Liu, would you please go to the side entrance? Your family is waiting for you there. 劉先生請到側門，您的家人在那裡等您。

關鍵句

Mr.Liu, would you please go to the side entrance? Your family is waiting for you there.

劉先生請到側門，您的家人在那裡等您。

應答語

Have you heard that, Mr.Liu? Hurry up to the side entrance.

劉先生，聽見了嗎？快去側門。

記憶提示

entrance：入口；side entrance：側門；front entrance：前門。

舉一反三

（1）Mr.Liu, somebody is waiting for you at the north gate. Please hurry up.
劉先生，有人在北門等您，快過去吧。

（2）Somebody is looking for you, Mr.Li.
李先生，有人正在找您。

107　Follow that arrow to the restroom. 洗手間在箭頭所指方向。

關鍵句

Follow that arrow to the restroom.

洗手間在箭頭所指方向。

Thank you.

謝謝。

記憶提示

arrow：箭，箭頭標誌。

restroom：洗手間、廁所，還可以說 washroom，bathroom 等。

舉一反三

（1）Follow that sign, and you can find the washroom.
順著那個標誌走，你就能找到洗手間了。

（2）Turn left, then you can get to the bathroom.
左轉就是洗手間。

108　This is a dead-end street. 這是個死胡同。

關鍵句

This is a dead-end street.

這是個死胡同。

Thanks for telling me.

謝謝你告訴我。

記憶提示

dead end：死巷；a dead-end street：盡頭街道，死胡同。

舉一反三

（1）Sorry, the street is a dead end.
抱歉，此路不通。

（2）I'm afraid you are in the wrong way.
恐怕你走錯路了。

109　Bottled water is 20 NT dollars each. 一瓶水 20 元錢。

關鍵句

How much is the bottled water?
一瓶水多少錢？

Bottled water is 20 NT dollars each.
一瓶水 20 元錢。

記憶提示

bottled water：瓶裝水；a bottle of water：一瓶水。

舉一反三

（1）Bottled water is much cheaper in the supermarket.
超市的瓶裝水便宜得多。

（2）It's 20 NT dollars for a bottle of water.
一瓶水 3 元錢。

110　You can buy films in the booth over there. 在那邊的亭子裡能買到底片。

關鍵句

You can buy films in the booth over there.
在那邊的亭子裡能買到底片。

Do they accept American money?

他們能收美元嗎？

記憶提示

film 除了有「電影」的意思，還有「膠捲、底片」的意思。如：see a film （看電影），buy a film （買底片）。

舉一反三

（1）You can buy films in the souvenir shop.

在紀念品店裡可以買到底片。

（2）I will let you know when I see a shop with films.

我要是看到哪個店裡有賣底片的，會告訴您的。

111　I've got a suntan. 我曬黑了。

關鍵句

I've got a suntan.

我曬黑了。

Don't worry. It doesn't look bad.

別擔心，看起來並不壞。

記憶提示

suntan ＝ tan：（皮膚的）曬黑；（使）曬成棕褐色。西方人很喜歡曬成棕褐色，夏天專門到海灘去曬太陽。

舉一反三

（1）I tan fast.

我一曬就黑。

（2）I need a hat to keep from suntan.

我需要一頂帽子，以免曬黑了。

112　Please keep an eye on the kids. 請看好您的孩子。

關鍵句

Please keep an eye on the kids.

請看好您的孩子。

It's very kind of you to remind me.

感謝您的善意提醒。

記憶提示

keep an eye on sb.：照顧（看）好某人。

舉一反三

（1）Catch hold of the kids in case they fall down.

拉著您的孩子，以免摔倒。

（2）Please take care of your children.

請看好您的孩子。

113　He is too young to climb the mountains. 他還太小，不能爬山。

關鍵句

He is too young to climb the mountains.

他還太小，不能爬山。

He may take a cable car up to the mountains.

他可以坐纜車上山。

記憶提示

too...to...：太⋯⋯而不能。

舉一反三

（1）I'm afraid he is so little that he can't climb the mountains.

我擔心他那麼小，不能爬山。

（2）It's hard for the little boy to climb the mountains.

爬山對這個小男孩來說很困難。

Unit 3　Sightseeing 觀光

Dialogue 典型對話示例

（ I ）

A：Would you like to recommend some places of interest?

您能為我推薦幾處名勝景點嗎？

B：OK. Terra-cotta horses and warriors in Xi'an are considered by some people as the eighth wonder in the world.

一些人認為西安兵馬俑是世界第八大奇蹟。

A：I think it absolutely is.

我認為那絕對是。

B：Suzhou's gardens are unique under heaven and West Lake in Hangzhou is a major scenic spot.

蘇州園林舉世無雙，杭州西湖是主要的景點。

A：Really! I won't miss them.

真的！我絕不能錯過。

B：Guilin's landscape is second to no one.

桂林山水甲天下。

A：I must go there when I have a chance.

我有機會一定會去的。

B：Murals in Dunhuang Grottoes make up an important part of world Buddhist culture.

敦煌壁畫是世界佛教文化的重要組成部分。

A：I'm eager to see them with my own eyes.

我太想去親眼看看了。

（ II ）

A：Beijing is a beautiful city with a lot of scenic spots and plac-es of his-torical interest.

北京是個有著許多風景名勝和歷史古蹟的城市。

B：We'd like to see as many as possible.

我們要儘量多看一些。

A：The Great Wall is one of the seven wonders of the world.

長城是世界七大奇蹟之一。

B：My heart aches for a visit already.

我已經迫不及待地想去參觀了。

A：Tian'anmen Square is the biggest city central square in the world.

天安門廣場是世界上最大的城市中心廣場。

B：I didn't realize it's so large.

我真沒想到它有這麼大。

A：The Summer Palace is famous for its beautiful scenery.

頤和園以風景美麗著稱。

B：I must take more pictures there.

我一定要在那兒多拍些照片。

A：The Palace Museum is worth seeing.

故宮很值得一看。

B：OK, we won't miss it.

好的，我們不會錯過的。

A：The Temple of Heaven is the place where the emperors of the Ming and Qing dynasties worshiped heaven and prayed for good harvest.

天壇是明清兩代皇帝祭天祈禱豐收的地方。

B：I guess it was a very important place for emperors.

我想對皇帝來說，那一定是非常重要的地方。

A：You're right. Yonghe Palace is a magnificent lama temple.

你說得對，雍和宮是一座很宏偉的喇嘛廟。

B：I'm very interested in Lamaism.

我對喇嘛教很感興趣。

（III）

A：Please keep an eye on your kids.

請照看好您的孩子。

B：Thank you for reminding me.

感謝您的提醒。

A：He is too young to climb the mountain.

他還太小，不能爬山。

B：What can I do?

那怎麼辦呢？

A：You may take a cable car up to the mountain.

您可以坐纜車上山。

B：OK. Where do I take it?

在哪裡坐纜車？

A：This way, please.

請這邊走。

Unit 4
Dining 飲食

Unit 4　Dining 飲食

重點單字

famous	famous 著名的
cuisine	（烹飪風格）菜系
dumpling	餃子
lunar year	農曆年
Cantonese food	粵菜
special	特別的
different	不同的
festival	節日
variety	種類、品種
snack	小吃
preserve	保藏，加工（食品等）
fruit	水果
specialty	特產
roast	烤
delicious	美味的
haw	山楂
sugar-coated haw	糖葫蘆
taste	品嚐
popular	流行的，受歡迎的
demonstrate	示範
restaurant	餐館
tomato	番茄
soup	湯
chopstick	筷子

distinguish	區別
attention	注意
freshness	新鮮
tenderness	嫩
smoothness	滑
spicy	辛辣的
feature	特徵
flavor	口味
pungent	辛辣的
salty	鹹的
fragrant	芳香的
sour	酸的
bitter	苦的
meat	（食用）肉
snake	蛇
attend	參加
order	點菜
pork	豬肉
prefer	更喜歡
occupy	占用
Mongolian	蒙古的
hot pot	火鍋
table d'hôte	套餐
à la carte	點菜
eight-jewel rice	八寶飯
dessert	餐後甜點

enjoy	滿意
satisfied	感到滿意的
bill	帳單
beverage	飲料
chief	主要的
pay	付款
cashier's	收銀處
check	支票
bar	酒吧
separate	分開的
customer	顧客
attract	吸引
roadside	路邊
potato	馬鈴薯
sell	賣
vendor	小販

Section I　Traditional Food 傳統食品

114　There are 8 famous cuisine in China. 中國有八大著名菜系。

關鍵句

There are 8 famous cuisins in China.

中國有八大著名菜系。

I love Cantonese food.

我喜愛粵菜。

記憶提示

cuisine：烹飪法；食品，伙食。

舉一反三

（1）There are 8 renowned dishes in China.
中國有八大著名菜系。

（2）There are 8 well-known foods in China.
中國有八大著名菜系。

115　Dumpling is a traditional food for Chinese New Year. 餃子是中國春節期間的一種傳統食物。

關鍵句

What is the main food for Chinese New Year?

中國春節的主要食物是什麼？

Dumpling is a traditional food for Chinese New Year.

餃子是中國春節期間的一種傳統食物。

記憶提示

Chinese New Year 即「中國新年」，或稱「中國春節（Chinese Spring Festival）」。

舉一反三

（1）Dumpling is the major food for Chinese New Year.

餃子是中國春節期間的主要食物。

（2）Dumpling is the chief food for Chinese New Year.

餃子是中國春節期間的主要食物。

116　Chinese eat different special food for different festivals. 華人在不同的節日會吃不同的特別食品。

關鍵句

Do Chinese have special food for different festivals?

華人在不同的節日會吃不同的食品嗎？

Yes. Chinese eat different special food for different festivals.

是的。華人在不同的節日會吃不同的特別食品。

記憶提示

Chinese 中國的，是專有集合名詞，可用作單數或複數，它是形容詞也是名詞。

舉一反三

Chinese celebrate particular festivals with diverse food.

華人在慶祝不同節日時有不同的食品。

117   There are many varieties of Taiwanese snacks. 臺灣有各種小吃。

關鍵句

How are the Taiwanese snacks?

臺灣的小吃怎麼樣？

There are many varieties of Taiwanese snacks.

臺灣有各種小吃。

記憶提示

snack：小吃；variety ＝ kind：種類。

舉一反三

There are various kinds of snacks in Taiwan.

臺灣有各種小吃。

118   Preserved fruits are Yilan specialty. 蜜餞是宜蘭的一種特產。

關鍵句

What is the available specialty in Yilan?

宜蘭有什麼特產？

Preserved fruits are Yilan specialty.

蜜餞是宜蘭的一種特產。

記憶提示

preserve 作動詞時，意為「（用冷凍、加工等方法）保藏（食品等）；（用醃製、蜜餞、醋漬、裝罐等方法）加工（食品等）」；作名詞時用複數形式，意為「（用醃製等方法）加工而成的食品（如蜜餞、果醬、罐頭等）」。candied：蜜餞的。

舉一反三

（1）Candied fruits are Yilan specialty.

蜜餞是宜蘭特產。

（2）Preserved fruit is special produce in Yilan.

蜜餞是宜蘭特產。

119　Roast Duck is very delicious. 烤鴨味道好極了。

關鍵句

How does the Roast Duck taste?

烤鴨味道怎麼樣？

Roast Duck is very delicious.

烤鴨味道好極了。

記憶提示

roast ＝ grill：燒烤；delicious 美味的，可口的。

舉一反三

（1）Roast Duck tastes good. 烤鴨味道好。

（2）Grilled Duck is yummy. 烤鴨味道好。

120　Sugar-coated haw on a stick tastes good. 糖葫蘆很好吃。

關鍵句

How is the taste of the sugar-coated haw?

糖葫蘆味道如何？

Sugar-coated haw on a stick tastes good.

糖葫蘆很好吃。

記憶提示

sugar-coated 作形容詞用，是「用糖包著」的意思。

舉一反三

Sugar-coated haw on a stick tastes delicious.

糖葫蘆很好吃。

121　Local vendors sell roast sweet potatoes on the roadside. 當地的小販沿街叫賣烤地瓜。

關鍵句

Local vendors sell roast sweet potatoes on the roadside.

當地的小販沿街叫賣烤地瓜。

It's tasty.

地瓜味道不錯。

記憶提示

roadside ＝ wayside：路邊，路旁。

舉一反三

（1）Local peddlers sell baked sweet potatoes by the wayside.

當地的小販沿街叫賣烤地瓜。

（2）Roast sweet potatoes are sold along the roadside.

街邊有賣烤地瓜的。

122　Shanghai food distinguishes itself with heavy sauce, thick soup and sweet taste. 上海菜以汁重、湯濃、味甜而著稱。

關鍵句

What does Shanghai food like?

上海菜的特點是什麼？

Shanghai food distinguishes itself with heavy sauce, thick soup and sweet taste.

上海菜以汁重、湯濃、味甜而著稱。

記憶提示

distinguish：區別，辨別；與 differ from 同義。

heavy sauce：濃湯。

舉一反三

（1）Shanghai food is characterized by its heavy sauce, thick soup and sweet taste.

上海菜以汁重、湯濃、味甜而著稱。

（2）Shanghai food is symbolized by its heavy sauce, thick soup and sweet taste.

上海菜以汁重、湯濃、味甜而著稱。

---

123 Cantonese cuisine pays great attention to the freshness, tenderness and smoothness of the dishes. 粵菜非常注重菜點的口感新鮮和嫩滑。

關鍵句

What is particular about Cantonese cuisine?

粵菜有什麼特色？

Cantonese cuisine pays great attention to the freshness, tenderness and smoothness of the dishes.

粵菜非常注重菜點的口感新鮮和嫩滑。

記憶提示

pay attention to sth. ＝ concentrate on sth.：注意、專心於某事。

舉一反三

Cantonese food usually tastes fresh, tender and smooth.

粵菜通常口感新鮮、嫩滑。

124　Sichuan food is usually very spicy. 川菜通常比較辣。

關鍵句

Sichuan food is usually very spicy.

川菜通常比較辣。

I enjoy spicy food.

我喜歡吃辣菜。

記憶提示

spicy ＝ hot：辛辣的。

舉一反三

Sichuan food is very hot.

川菜非常辣。

125　Sichuan cuisine features the seven flavors —— hot, pungent, sour, bitter, sweet, salty and fragrant. 川菜以熱、辣、苦、甜、鹹和香為特色。

關鍵句

What are the characteristics of Sichuan cuisine?

川菜有什麼特色？

Sichuan cuisine features the seven flavors —— hot, pungent, sour, bitter, sweet, salty and fragrant.

川菜以熱、辣、苦、甜、鹹和香為特色。

記憶提示

flavor ＝ savor：滋味。

舉一反三

（1）Sichuan food has the seven flavors ── hot, pungent, sour, bitter, sweet, salty and fragrant.

川菜以熱、辣、苦、甜、鹹和香為特色。

（2）Sichuan style cuisine is known for the seven flavors ── hot, pungent, sour, bitter, sweet, salty and fragrant.

川菜以熱、辣、苦、甜、鹹和香為特色。

---

126 Some people eat dog meat and snake meat. 有些人吃狗肉和蛇肉。

關鍵句

Some people eat dog meat and snake meat.

有些人吃狗肉和蛇肉。

It's terrible.

太可怕了。

記憶提示

flesh：肉，（供食用的）獸肉，人體。

meat：（食用）肉，肉類。

舉一反三

Some people enjoy dog meat and snake meat.

有些人喜歡吃狗肉和蛇肉。

Unit 4　Dining 飲食

127　Chinese tea is one of the chief beverages in the world. 中國茶是世界主要飲料之一。

關鍵句

Chinese tea is one of the chief beverages in the world.

中國茶是世界主要飲料之一。

I love Chinese tea.

我愛喝中國茶。

記憶提示

beverage = drink：飲料，如茶、酒、牛奶、汽水、低卡汽水等。

舉一反三

（1）Chinese tea is one of the main drinks in the world.

中國茶是世界主要飲料之一。

（2）Chinese tea is gaining popularity in the world.

中國茶在世界上越來越盛行。

Section II　Having Meals 用餐

128.The bar street attracts a lot of customers. 酒吧街吸引了很多顧客。

關鍵句

The bar street attracts a lot of customers.

酒吧街吸引了很多顧客。

It's a busy street.

這是一條繁忙的街道。

記憶提示

bar：酒吧間； bar street：酒吧街。

舉一反三

（1） Many people like to go to the bar street.
酒吧街吸引了大量顧客。

（2） The bar street draws lot of customers.
酒吧街吸引了大量顧客。

129 It's time for lunch. 該吃午飯了。

關鍵句

It's time for lunch.

該吃午飯了。

Yes, it's almost 12 o'clock.

是啊，已經快 12 點了。

記憶提示

lunch 是午餐，luncheon 指正式的午餐、午宴。

舉一反三

（1） It's our lunch time now.
該吃午飯了。

（2） Let's take a lunch break.
我們該吃午飯了。

130　Where is the nearest restaurant? 最近的餐廳在哪裡？

關鍵句

Where is the nearest restaurant?

最近的餐廳在哪裡？

It's at the corner of this street.

就在這條街的轉角處。

記憶提示

near：近的；其比較級形式是 nearer（較近的）；nearest（最近的）是其最高級形式。

舉一反三

Where is the neighboring restaurant?

最近的餐廳在哪裡？

131　I'd like to reserve a table for four at 6 o'clock this evening. 我想預訂一張四人桌，晚上 6 點過去。

關鍵句

I'd like to reserve a table for four at 6 o'clock this evening.

我想預訂一張四人桌，晚上 6 點過去。

OK. May I have your name？

好的。請問您貴姓？

記憶提示

reserve ＝ book ＝ order：預訂。

舉一反三

May I have a table for four at 6 o'clock this evening?

我想預訂今晚 6 點一張四人桌，可以嗎？

132.How large is your party? 您有幾位？

關鍵句

How large is your party?

您有幾位？

We have four people.

我們四個人。

記憶提示

（1）large 和 big 都有「大」的意思，通常可互換使用。但 big 多用於指體
積、規模、重量、程度方面的大；large 通常指寬度、數量之大。

（2）party 在這裡的意思是「團體、群」，不是「派對、晚會」的意思，
回答時應是一個數字。

舉一反三

（1）How big is your party?
您有幾位？

（2）How many people are there in your party?
您有幾位？

133　Are you being attended to? 有人招呼您了嗎？

關鍵句

Are you being attended to?

有人招呼您了嗎？

Yes, I am. Thank you.

是的。謝謝。

記憶提示

attend to ＝ wait on：招待。

舉一反三

（1）Are you being waited on?

有人招呼您了嗎？

（2）Are you being served?

有人招呼您了嗎？

134　Which table would you prefer? 您想坐什麼位置？

關鍵句

Which table would you prefer?

您想坐什麼位置？

I prefer this one.

我想坐這裡。

記憶提示

prefer：更喜歡、寧願，在這句子裡可用 like 代替。

舉一反三

（1）Which table would you like?
　　您想坐哪裡？

（2）Which table do you want?
　　您喜歡坐什麼位置？

135　Is this table occupied? 這張桌子有人嗎？

關鍵句

Is this table occupied?

這張桌子有人嗎？

Yes, it is occupied.

有人。

記憶提示

occupy 在這裡是「占用」的意思。

舉一反三

（1）Is this table vacant?
　　這張桌子有人嗎？

（2）Is this table for anybody else?
　　這張桌子有人嗎？

136　Are you ready to order? 可以點菜了嗎？

關鍵句

Are you ready to order?

可以點菜了嗎？

Yes, I am ready.

可以了。

記憶提示

（1）order dish：點菜； order 作動詞時，常用來表示在飯店點菜，還可以作名詞，表示「所點的菜」。

（2）be ready （for sth./to do sth.）表示準備的狀態，get ready （for sth./to do sth.）表示準備的動作。

舉一反三

（1）Are you prepared to order?

可以點菜了嗎？

（2）Are you getting ready to order?

可以點菜了嗎？

137　Would you like a set menu or à la carte? 您要吃套餐還是單點？

關鍵句

Would you like a set menu or à la carte?

您要吃套餐還是單點？

I prefer à la carte.

我要單點。

記憶提示

a set menu：客飯菜單，套餐菜單，與 table d'hôte 同義；à la carte：按菜單點菜，此詞來自法語。

舉一反三

（1）Do you prefer table d'hôte or à la carte?

你要套餐還是單點？

（2）Will you dine à la carte or take a set menu?

您要單點呢，還是吃套餐？

138 Would you show us how to eat Roast Duck? 教我們如何吃烤鴨，好嗎？

關鍵句

Would you show us how to eat Roast Duck?

教我們如何吃烤鴨，好嗎？

It's a pleasure.

榮幸之至。

記憶提示

eat：吃。在家吃飯可說「eat in」，上館子是「eat out」。

舉一反三

（1）Would you demonstrate how to eat Roast Duck?

請你示範一下怎樣吃烤鴨好嗎？

（2）Please tell us how to eat Roast Duck.
請告訴我們怎樣吃烤鴨。

139　We would like to learn to use chopsticks. 我們想學學 如何用筷子。

關鍵句

We would like to learn to use chopsticks.
我們想學學如何用筷子。

I'm glad to teach you.
我很高興教你們。

記憶提示

learn：學習；learn of（about）：獲知。

舉一反三

（1）We'd like to learn how to eat with chopsticks.
我們想學用筷子吃飯。

（2）We'd like to learn to deal with chopsticks.
我們想學使用筷子。

140　Would you like sweet and sour pork? 您想吃咕咾肉 嗎？

關鍵句

Would you like sweet and sour pork?
您想吃咕咾肉嗎？

Is it good?

好吃嗎？

記憶提示

酸、甜、苦、辣、鹹的英文分別是 sour, sweet, bitter, spicy （hot）,salty。
咕咾肉的味道為酸甜（sweet and sour）摻半。

舉一反三

（1）Would you fancy sweet and sour pork?

您喜歡吃咕咾肉嗎？

（2）Do you want sweet and sour pork?

您要吃咕咾肉嗎？

141 How about Mongolian hotpot? 吃火鍋（涮羊肉）如何？

關鍵句

How about Mongolian hotpot?

吃火鍋（涮羊肉）如何？

It sounds nice.

聽起來不錯。

記憶提示

Mongolian hotpot ＝ rinse mutton in hotpot with boiling water or soup：
涮羊肉。

Unit 4　Dining 飲食

Don't you like Mongolian hotpot?

您不喜歡火鍋（涮羊肉）嗎？

142　Would you like to have some dessert? 要來點什麼甜食嗎？

關鍵句

Would you like to have some dessert?

要來點什麼甜食嗎？

Sure.

好啊。

記憶提示

dessert：餐後甜品，可以是水果，也可以是糕點之類。

注意：desert（沙漠）與 dessert 只是一個字母之差，但發音、意思都不同。

舉一反三

（1）What dessert do you like to have?

來點什麼甜食？

（2）Do you need to have some dessert?

您需要來點什麼甜食嗎？

143 What would you like to drink? 你們想喝點什麼？

關鍵句

What would you like to drink?

你們想喝點什麼？

I would like a glass of orange juice.

我想要一杯柳橙汁。

記憶提示

drink 作動詞時是「喝」的意思，作名詞時指「酒水、飲料」。

舉一反三

（1）What drink would you like?

你們想喝點什麼？

（2）What do you want to drink?

你們想喝點什麼？

144 Sour and spicy soup tastes good. 酸辣湯味道不錯。

關鍵句

Sour and spicy soup tastes good.

酸辣湯味道不錯。

Yes, I think so.

是的，我也這樣認為。

記憶提示

sour and spicy soup：酸辣湯，是由胡椒粉、雞蛋、豆製品、澱粉、水等做成。

舉一反三

（1）Sour and spicy soup tastes nice.
　　酸辣湯味道很好。

（2）Sour and spicy soup is delicious.
　　酸辣湯味道很可口。

145　Would you like some local food? 您想嚐一下本地口味的菜嗎？

關鍵句

Would you like some local food?

您想嚐一下本地口味的菜嗎？

Yes, I should have some.

好啊！我應該嚐一下本地菜。

記憶提示

local food ＝ native food：本地菜餚。

舉一反三

Would you like some local dishes?

您想點些本地口味的菜嗎？

146　Is there anything else you would like to have? 您還需要別的嗎？

關鍵句

Is there anything else you would like to have?

您還需要別的嗎？

No, nothing else.

不需要什麼了。

記憶提示

注意：else 要放在 anything, nothing, something 之後，與中文表述的詞序正好相反。

舉一反三

（1）Anything more you want to have?

您還需要點什麼嗎？

（2）Do you need anything else?

您還需要點什麼嗎？

147　Enjoy your meal. 您請慢用。

關鍵句

Enjoy your meal.

您請慢用。

Thank you.

謝謝。

記憶提示

enjoy：享受……的樂趣，欣賞，喜愛。

meal：一餐，一頓飯。

148　I am full. 我吃飽了。

關鍵句

I am full.

我吃飽了。

記憶提示

full：飽的，吃漲的。

舉一反三

I've eaten and drunk to my full.

我已經吃飽喝足了。

Section III　Paying the Bill 結帳

149.Bill, please. 買單。

關鍵句

Bill, please.

買單。

One moment, please.

請稍候。

記憶提示

bill：帳單，也可用 check 表示。

舉一反三

Bring me the bill, please.

我要結帳。

150 Will that be separate checks or one? 一起付還是分開付？

關鍵句

Will that be separate checks or one?

一起付還是分開付？

We will pay separately.

我們要分開付。

記憶提示

separate 可用作動詞或形容詞，但發音不盡相同。

舉一反三

（1）Will you pay respectively or in one check?

一起付還是分開付？

（2）Are there separate checks or one ？

一起付還是分開付？

151 Please pay at the cashier's. 請到收銀處付款。

關鍵句

Please pay at the cashier's.

請到收銀處付款。

OK.

好的。

記憶提示

cashier：出納員；at the cashier's：在收銀處。

舉一反三

（1）Please go to the cashier's.

請到收銀處付款。

（2）Please give money at the cashier's.

請到收銀處付款。

152　Service charge is not included. 服務費沒有包括在內。

關鍵句

Service charge is not included.

服務費沒有包括在內。

I see.

我知道了。

舉一反三

Service charge is excluded.

服務費沒有包括在內。

Dialogue 典型對話示例

（Ⅰ）

A：Do Chinese have special food for different festivals?

華人在不同的節日都吃特別的食物嗎？

B：Yes, they have different special food for different festivals.

是的，華人在不同的節日都有不同的特製食物。

A：What is the traditional food for the Chinese New Year?

中國春節期間的傳統食品是什麼？

B：It's dumpling.

是餃子。

A：Have you tasted any Taiwanese snacks?

您品嚐過什麼臺灣小吃了嗎？

B：Yes, but only some of them. There are so many varieties of Taiwanese snacks.

已經嚐過了一些。臺灣的小吃種類太多了。

A：You're absolutely right.

您說得太對了。

（Ⅱ）

A：Waiter, bring me the bill, please.

服務生，我要買單。

B：Will that be separate checks or one?

一起付還是分開付？

A：We will pay separately.

我們要分開付。

B：OK, please wait a moment. I'll be right back with your bill.

好的，請稍等，我馬上把帳單拿過來。

（The waiter brings the bill.）

（服務生拿來了帳單。）

Here is the bill. Have you enjoyed your meal?

這是帳單。您今天用餐還滿意嗎？

A：Yes, it's not bad.

是的，還不錯。

B：Thank you. Please come again.

謝謝您。歡迎您再次光臨。

Unit 5
Accommodations 住宿

Unit 5　Accommodations 住宿

重點單字

different	不同的
star-rated hotel	星級飯店
book	預訂
locate	坐落
in the center of	在中心
front desk	櫃檯
reservation	預訂
name	名字
spell	拼寫
be from	來自……
passport	護照
fill out	填寫
registration card/form	登記表
sign one's name	簽名
kind	種類
king size	標準大床
twin beds	兩張單人床
smoke	吸菸
non-smoking	不吸菸的
face the lake	面向湖
payment	付款
imprint	留下烙印
credit card	信用卡
check out time	退房時間

noon	中午
breakfast	早餐
room card	房卡
breakfast coupon	早餐券
morning call	叫醒服務
bellboy	行李員
help	幫助
baggage	行李
elevator	電梯
indoor swimming pool	室內游泳池
brochure	小冊子
drawer	抽屜
conference room	會議室
second floor	二樓
function room	多功能廳
room service	送餐到房間的服務
cold	冷的
blanket	毯子
extra bed	加床
clean	打掃
repair	修理
right now	馬上
laundry	要洗的衣服
shirt	襯衫
starched	漿硬的
pick up	拾取

garment	衣服
wash by hand	手洗
cold water	冷水
shrink	收縮
otherwise	否則
stain	汙漬
spill	灑
soy sauce	醬油
put through	接過去
hold on	不要掛斷
number	號碼
engaged	忙碌的
leave a message	留言
again	再次
later	稍後
collect call	對方付費電話
area code	電話區號
U.K.	英國
pay call	直接付費電話
exchange rate	兌幣匯率
US dollar	美元
exchange memo	兌幣水單
provide	提供
fax	傳真
internet services	上網服務
several	幾個

choose from	選擇
since	因為
water pipe	水管
repair	修理
available	可用到的
9:00 a.m.	上午九點
4:00 p.m.	下午四點
water tap	水龍頭
drip	滴
all night	一夜
sleep	睡覺
toilet	盥洗室；馬桶
flush	沖水
clog	阻塞
bathtub	浴缸
leak	洩漏
fix	修理
air conditioner	空調
broken	壞掉的
electric light	電燈
out of order	壞了
room number	房間號碼
cakes of soap	幾塊肥皂
stay up late	熬夜
extend	延伸
check out	退房

bill	帳單
total	總的
change	找回的零錢
receipt	收據
make sure	確保

Section I Hotel Booking & Check-in 預訂飯店及登記入住

153　There are different star-rated hotels in Taipei. 臺北有各種星級飯店。

關鍵句

There are different star-rated hotels in Taipei.

臺北有各種星級飯店。

Are they up to the standard?

它們都達到標準了嗎？

記憶提示

hotel 是「旅館、飯店」，是住宿和吃飯的地方。restaurant 餐館、飯店，是吃飯的地方。hostel 是青年旅館，inn 是小旅館，motel 是汽車旅館。

舉一反三

There are various star-rated hotels in Taipei.

臺北有各種星級飯店。

---

154 Which hotel would you like to reserve? 您想要預訂哪家飯店？

關鍵句

Which hotel would you like to reserve?

您想要預訂哪家飯店？

I would like to book the East Hotel.

我要預訂東方飯店。

舉一反三

Which hotel would you like to stay at?

您想要住哪家飯店？

---

155 Your hotel is located in the center of Taipei. 你們下榻的飯店坐落在臺北市中心。

關鍵句

Your hotel is located in the center of Taipei.

你們下榻的飯店坐落在臺北市中心。

Yes, it's convenient.

是的，很方便。

記憶提示

located = situated：處於，位於。

舉一反三

（1）Your hotel is situated in the center of Taipei.
你們下榻的飯店坐落在臺北市中心。

（2）Your hotel stands in the center of Beijing.
你們下榻的飯店坐落在臺北市中心。

156　Do you have a reservation with us? 您有預訂嗎？

關鍵句

Do you have a reservation with us?

您有預訂嗎？

Yes, I have.

有預訂。

記憶提示

reservation = advance booking：預訂。

舉一反三

（1）Have you got a reservation?
您有預訂嗎？

（2）Do you have an advance booking?
您有預訂嗎？

157 May I have your name? 請問您貴姓？

關鍵句

May I have your name?

請問您貴姓？

My name is John Smith.

我的名字是約翰‧史密斯。

舉一反三

（1）What's your name, please?

請問您貴姓？

（2）May I know your name?

請問您貴姓？

158 Could you spell your name? 請拼寫一下您的名字，好嗎？

關鍵句

Could you spell your name?

請拼寫一下您的名字，好嗎？

My name is John Smith, J-O-H-N, John, S-M-I-T-H, Smith.

我叫約翰‧史密斯，J-O-H-N，John，S-M-I-T-H，Smith。

記憶提示

spell：拼寫。名詞形式為 spelling。當沒有聽清對方姓名，不知如何拼寫時，可用此句型。

159　Where are you from? 您是哪裡人？

關鍵句

Where are you from?

您是哪裡人？

I'm from Australia.

我是澳洲人。

記憶提示

「Where are you from」直譯是「您從哪裡來」，也就是「您是哪裡人」。

舉一反三

Where do you come from?

您是哪裡人？

160　May I see your passport? 可以看一下您的護照嗎？

關鍵句

May I see your passport?

可以看一下您的護照嗎？

Here it is.

好的。

記憶提示

passport：護照。護照是一個國家的公民到別的國家時必須持有的證件，以證明自己的身分。

舉一反三

May I have a look at your passport?

可以看一下您的護照嗎？

---

161 Would you please fill out the registration form? 請您填寫一下登記表。

關鍵句

Would you please fill out the registration form?

請您填寫一下登記表。

Certainly.

好的。

記憶提示

fill out ＝ fill in：填寫；registration form：登記卡，入住飯店時一般都要填寫登記卡。填寫項目大概有姓名、年齡、性別、國籍、永久居住地的地址等。

舉一反三

Would you please fill in the registration card?

請您填寫一下登記表。

162　Will you please sign your name here? 請您在這裡簽名。

關鍵句

Will you please sign your name here?

請您在這裡簽名。

Is it right here?

是在這裡嗎？

記憶提示

sign = write down one's signature：簽名。

舉一反三

（1）Will you please write your name here?

請您在此簽名。

（2）Will you please put down your signature here?

請您在此簽名。

163　What kind of room do you want? 您想要哪種房間？

關鍵句

What kind of room do you want?

您想要哪種房間？

I'd like a single room.

我要一間單人房。

記憶提示

飯店的房間有總統套房（presidential suite）、套房（suite room）、雙人房（double room）、單人房（single room）、可吸菸房間（smoking room）和不可吸菸房間（non-smoking room）等。

舉一反三

What type of room do you prefer?

您想要哪種房間？

164　Do you want a king-size bed or twin beds? 您想要標準大床房還是雙人標準房？

關鍵句

Do you want a king-size bed or twin beds?

您想要標準大床房還是雙人標準房？

I want a king-size one.

我要標準大床房。

記憶提示

飯店房間的房型不同，床的尺寸也有所不同。通常有如下幾種：king-size bed（標準大床），queen-size bed（大號床），twin beds（兩張單人床），single bed（單人床）。

舉一反三

Do you request a king-size bed or twin beds?

您要標準大床房還是雙人標準房？

165　Would you like a smoking room or non-smoking room? 您要可吸菸房還是不可吸菸房？

關鍵句

Would you like a smoking room or non-smoking room?

您要可吸菸房還是不可吸菸房？

I'd like a non-smoking room.

我要非吸菸房。

記憶提示

non-smoking：不可吸菸的。non- 作為前綴，表示否定作用，如 non-alcoholic（不含酒精的）。

舉一反三

（1）Do you like a smoking or non-smoking room?

您要可吸菸房還是不可吸菸房？

（2）Would you want a smoking or non-smoking room?

您要可吸菸房還是不可吸菸房？

166　I'd like a room facing the lake. 我要面向湖的房間。

關鍵句

I'd like a room facing the lake.

我要面向湖的房間。

There is one on the second floor.

二樓有一間。

記憶提示

英語中只有河（river）、湖（lake）、海（sea）、海洋（ocean），而沒有「江」這個詞，通常用 river 一詞來表示。如：The Yangtze River（長江）。

舉一反三

I'd like a room with lake view.
我想要能望見湖的房間。

167 How would you like your payment? 您用哪種方式結帳？

關鍵句

How would you like your payment?
您用哪種方式結帳？
I would like to pay by traveler's check.
我想用旅行支票付。

記憶提示

結帳的方式有多種，可使用個人支票（with a personal check）、現金（in cash）、信用卡（by credit card）、旅行支票（with a traveler's check）等。

舉一反三

How would you like to pay?
您用哪種方式結帳？

168 May I take an imprint of your credit card? 我刷一下您的信用卡好嗎？

關鍵句

May I take an imprint of your credit card?

我刷一下您的信用卡好嗎？

Yes, please.

好的。

記憶提示

credit card：信用卡，credit 是信譽，card 是卡；它攜帶方便，掉失可向發卡公司掛失，比現金保險，是世界各國使用普遍的付款方式。

舉一反三

Can I take an imprint of your credit card?

我刷一下您的信用卡好嗎？

169 The checkout time is before noon. 退房時間是中午 12 點以前。

關鍵句

The checkout time is before noon.

退房時間是中午 12 點以前。

OK, I'll check out before noon。

好的，我會在中午前退房。

記憶提示

checkout time：退房時間；check in：入住飯店。

舉一反三

Time for check out is before noon.

退房時間是中午 12 點以前。

170　Breakfast is included in the price. 費用中包含早餐。

關鍵句

Breakfast is included in the price.

費用中包含早餐。

That's good.

那好啊。

記憶提示

早餐：breakfast，有些飯店房費裡包含早餐，也有不包含的。

舉一反三

（1）Breakfast is contained in the price.

房費中包含早餐。

（2）Breakfast is covered in the price.

房費中包含早餐。

171　Here are your room card and breakfast coupon. 這是您的房卡和早餐券。

關鍵句

Here are your room card and breakfast coupon.

這是您的房卡和早餐券。

Thank you.

謝謝。

記憶提示

room card：房卡，是客人到櫃檯取鑰匙的證明，有些房卡可作鑰匙用。

breakfast coupon：早餐券，是客人在飯店用早餐的證明。

舉一反三

These are your room card and breakfast coupon.

這是您的房卡和早餐券。

172　Do you need a morning call? 您需要叫醒服務嗎？

關鍵句

Do you need a morning call?

您需要叫醒服務嗎？

Yes, I do.

是的，我需要。

記憶提示

morning call ＝ wake-up call：叫醒服務。

舉一反三

（1）Would you like a morning call?

您需要叫醒服務嗎？

（2）Do you want a wake-up call?

您需要叫醒服務嗎？

173 The bellboy will show you to your room. 行李員會帶您去房間。

關鍵句

The bellboy will show you to your room.

行李員會帶您去房間。

OK, thank you.

好的，謝謝。

記憶提示

bellboy ＝ porter：行李員。

舉一反三

The porter will lead you to your room.

行李員會帶您去房間。

Unit 5 Accommodations 住宿

174 May I help you with your luggage? 要我幫您提行李嗎？

關鍵句

May I help you with your luggage?

要我幫您提行李嗎？

That's very kind of you.

那太好了。

記憶提示

help sb. with sth.：幫助某人做某事。

舉一反三

Shall I take the baggage for you?

我幫您提行李好嗎？

175 Here is the elevator. 這裡是電梯了。

關鍵句

Here is the elevator. You first.

這裡是電梯了。您先請。

記憶提示

elevator〈主美〉 = lift〈主英〉：電梯。

舉一反三

This is the elevator.

電梯在這裡。

176. After you. 您先請。

關鍵句

After you.

您先請。

Thank you.

謝謝。

記憶提示

目前國際通行的禮儀慣例是「女士優先」、「長者先行」。用英文表述分別是「Lady first」和「Age before beauty」。

舉一反三

You first.

您先請。

Section II Hotel Facilities & Service 飯店設施與服務

177.Is there an indoor swimming pool in the hotel? 飯店有室內游泳池嗎？

關鍵句

Is there an indoor swimming pool in the hotel?

飯店有室內游泳池嗎？

Yes. It's on the third floor.

有，在三樓。

記憶提示

indoor swimming pool：室內游泳池； indoor stadium：室內體育館。

舉一反三

（1）Do you have an indoor swimming pool in the hotel?
飯店有室內游泳池嗎？

（2）Is there an indoor swimming pool available in the hotel?
飯店有室內游泳池嗎？

178　Our hotel brochure is in the drawer. 飯店服務手冊在抽屜裡。

關鍵句

Our hotel brochure is in the drawer.

飯店服務手冊在抽屜裡。

I'll read it.

我會看的。

記憶提示

brochure ＝ pamphlet：小冊子。

舉一反三

（1）You may find our hotel pamphlet in the drawer.
您可以在抽屜裡找到我們飯店的服務手冊。

（2）There is a brochure on our hotel inside the drawer.
抽屜裡有我們飯店的服務手冊。

179 The conference rooms are on the second floor. 會議室在二樓。

關鍵句

The conference rooms are on the second floor.

會議室在二樓。

It was said that the facilities in the conference room are great.

據說會議室的設備很棒。

記憶提示

conference room ＝ meeting room：會議室。

second floor 在臺灣和美國指二樓，在英國則是指三樓。

舉一反三

The meeting rooms are on the second floor.

會議室在二樓。

180 We have several conference rooms for you to choose from. 我們有好幾間會議室供您選擇。

關鍵句

We have several conference rooms for you to choose from.

我們有好幾間會議室供您選擇。

We'd like to hire the one on the fourth floor.

我們想租用第四層的那間。

記憶提示

conference room ＝ meeting room：會議室。

舉一反三

There are several conference rooms for you to select.

我們有好幾間會議室供您選擇。

181　We provide fax and Internet services. 我們提供傳真和上網服務。

關鍵句

We provide fax and Internet services.

我們提供傳真和上網服務。

That's really convenient.

那真方便。

記憶提示

provide：供應，供給；Internet：網際網路，國際互聯網。

舉一反三

（1）We supply fax and Internet services.

我們提供傳真和上網服務。

（2）Fax and Internet services are available.

我們提供傳真和上網服務。

182 The exchange rate today is 30.74 NT dollars to one US dollar. 今天的匯率是 1 美元兌新臺幣 30.74 元。

關鍵句

The exchange rate today is 30.74 NT dollars to one US dollar.

今天的匯率是 1 美元兌新臺幣 30.74 元。

It is higher than yesterday.

匯率比昨天高了。

記憶提示

exchange rate：匯率；新臺幣：NT dollars；美元：US dollar；日元：Yen。

舉一反三

The exchange rate today is one US dollar to 30.74 NT dollars.

今天的匯率是 1 美元兌新臺幣 30.74 元。

183 How would you like your money? 您要什麼面額的？

關鍵句

How would you like your money?

您要什麼面額的？

I would like ten 100 dollars notes.

我想要 10 張 100 元面額的紙幣。

記憶提示

money：錢；（錢的）面額：denomination。

舉一反三

In what denomination?

您要什麼面額的？

184   Please keep your exchange memo safe. 請您保存好兌幣收據。

關鍵句

Please keep your exchange memo safe.

請您保存好兌換收據。

What do I keep it for?

我留著它有什麼用嗎？

記憶提示

memo：備忘錄，這裡指收據（receipt）。

185   Can you tell me the way to the function room, please? 請問去多功能廳怎麼走？

關鍵句

Can you please tell me the way to the function room, please?

請問去多功能廳怎麼走？

This way, please.

請這邊走。

記憶提示

way：路，路線，道路；常與介詞 to 連用。

舉一反三

(1) Could you please tell me where the function room is?

請問去多功能廳怎麼走？

(2) Could you please show me the way to the function room?

請問去多功能廳怎麼走？

186　Do you have room service? 你們有客房送餐服務嗎？

關鍵句

Do you have room service?

你們有客房送餐服務嗎？

Yes, we do.

我們有。

記憶提示

room service：（飯店裡的）客房用膳送餐服務。一般費用較高，但有些客人因為各種原因不能去餐廳用餐，所以需要送餐服務。

舉一反三

(1) Have you got room service?

你們有客房送餐服務嗎？

(2) Is there room service in your hotel?

你們有客房送餐服務嗎？

187　Would you please send the breakfast to Room 101? 請把早餐送到 101 房間，好嗎？

關鍵句

Would you please send the breakfast to Room 101?

請把早餐送到 101 房間，好嗎？

It will be sent to your room right away.

早餐將馬上送到你的房間去。

記憶提示

早餐：breakfast；午餐：lunch；晚餐：dinner；早午餐：brunch ［指早午兩餐併到一起吃，即 br(eakfast) ＋ (l)unch］。

舉一反三

Would you please deliver the breakfast to Room 101?

請把早餐送到 101 房間。

188　Room service. May I come in? 送餐服務，可以進房嗎？

關鍵句

Room service. May I come in?

送餐服務，可以進房嗎？

Come in, please.

請進。

記憶提示

此處服務員說「Room service」是在其敲客人房門時的自報家門，這是規範服務的一個重要環節。

189　It's too cold. I need another blanket. 太冷了，我需要加條毯子。

關鍵句

It is too cold. I need another blanket.

太冷了，我需要加條毯子。

I'll send it to you as soon as possible.

我會盡快給你送去。

記憶提示

blanket：毯子。加毯子一般是不加收費用的，但在國外往往需要給送毯子的服務員小費。

舉一反三

（1）It's too cold. I need one more blanket.

太冷了，我需要加條毯子。

（2）It's too cold. I'd like another blanket.

太冷了，我需要加條毯子。

190　We need an extra bed in Room 202. 202 房間需要加張床。

關鍵句

We need an extra bed in Room 202.

202 房間需要加張床。

OK. It will be put into your room in a moment.

好的。馬上就會送進您房間的。

記憶提示

extra bed：加床。這項服務一般是要收費的，但收費標準各飯店有所不同。

舉一反三

（1）We want an extra bed in Room 202.
202 房間需要加張床。

（2）An extra bed is needed in Room 202.
202 房間需要加張床。

191　My room number is 2066. Please send me some bars of soap. 我的房間號是 2066，請幫我送幾塊肥皂來。

關鍵句

My room number is 2066. Please send me some bars of soap.

我的房間號是 2066，請幫我送幾塊肥皂來。

Just a minute, please.

請稍等。

記憶提示

bar：酒吧；條，（長形或橢圓形的）塊。如：a bar of gold：金條；a bar of chocolate：一塊條形巧克力。

舉一反三

We need some bars of soap in room 2066.

2066 房間需要幾塊肥皂。

Section III Housekeeping & Laundry Service 客房清潔及洗衣服務

192 May I clean your room now? 現在可以打掃您的房間嗎？

關鍵句

May I clean your room now?

現在可以打掃您的房間嗎？

Sure.

當然可以。

記憶提示

clean：既可作動詞也可作形容詞，意為「打掃，使乾淨；乾淨的」。

例：keep one's room clean：（保持房間乾淨），clean one's room：（打掃房間）。

> **193** Since the water pipes are being repaired, cold water isn't available from 9:00 a.m. to 4:00 p.m. 由於水管檢修，早上 9 點到下午 4 點要停水。

關鍵句

Since the water pipes are being repaired, cold water isn't available from 9:00 a.m. to 4:00 p.m.

由於水管檢修，早上 9 點到下午 4 點要停水。

That's too bad.

太糟糕了。

記憶提示

water pipe 是水管，自來水是 tap water 或 running water。

舉一反三

（1）Since the water pipes are being repaired, cold water supply would cut off from 9:00 a.m. to 4:00 p.m.

由於水管檢修，早上 9 點到下午 4 點停水。

（2）Since the water pipes are being repaired, cold water supply will stop from 9:00 a.m. to 4:00 p.m.

由於水管檢修，早上 9 點到下午 4 點停水。

> **194** I have some laundry to be done. 我有一些衣服要洗。

關鍵句

I have some laundry to be done.

我有一些衣服要洗。

You can have them back tomorrow afternoon.

明天下午給您送回來。

記憶提示

laundry：洗衣店，要洗的衣服，洗熨。

舉一反三

（1）I'd like to have some laundry done.

我有一些衣服要洗。

（2）I have some laundry.

我有一些衣服要洗。

195　The shirts have to be starched. 這些襯衫要漿一下。

關鍵句

The shirts have to be starched.

這些襯衫要漿一下。

We can do a good job.

我們會把這些襯衫漿好的。

記憶提示

shirt：男式襯衫；blouse：女式襯衫。

舉一反三

（1）The shirts need to be starched.

這些襯衫要漿一下。

（2）The shirts must be starched.

這些襯衫要漿一下。

> **196**　I'll pick up your laundry right now. 我馬上去取您要洗的衣物。

關鍵句

I'll pick up your laundry right now.

我馬上去取您要洗的衣物。

When can I have them back?

什麼時候能給我送回來？

記憶提示

pick up：取（某物），接（某人）。

舉一反三

I'll go and get them immediately.

我馬上去取您要洗的衣物。

> **197**　I'd like this garment to be washed by hand in cold water. It might shrink otherwise. 這件衣服要用冷水手洗，不然可能會縮水。

關鍵句

I'd like this garment to be washed by hand in cold water. It might shrink otherwise.

這件衣服要用冷水手洗，不然可能會縮水。

Yes, I see.

好的，我明白了。

記憶提示

cold 是冷，cool 是涼快，warm 是暖和，hot 是熱。

舉一反三

（1）I'd like this garment not to be washed by machine. It might shrink otherwise.

這件衣服不要用機器洗，不然可能會縮水。

（2）I'd like this garment to be washed by hand in cold water in case it might shrink.

這件衣服要用冷水手洗，以免縮水。

198 What kind of stain is it on the shirt? 襯衫上是什麼汙漬？

關鍵句

What kind of stain is it on the shirt?

襯衫上是什麼汙漬？

It's stained with ink.

是墨水汙漬。

記憶提示

stain 作名詞指「汙點、瑕疵」；作動詞指「弄髒、汙染、玷汙」。

舉一反三

（1）What kind of smirch is it on the shirt?

襯衫上是什麼汙漬？

（2）What sort of dirt is it on the shirt?

襯衫上是什麼汙漬？

199　I spilled some soy sauce on it. 我灑了點醬油在上面。

關鍵句

I spilled some soy sauce on it.
我灑了點醬油在上面。
I will wash it for you.
我會幫您洗乾淨。

記憶提示

spill＝splash：濺出。

舉一反三

（1）I splashed some soy sauce on it.
　　 我灑了點醬油在上面。

（2）I sprinkled some soy sauce on it.
　　 我灑了點醬油在上面。

Section Ⅳ　Problems in the Guestroom 客房設施故障問題

200　Is your room OK? 您的房間沒什麼問題吧？

關鍵句

Is your room OK?
您的房間沒什麼問題吧？

Yes, it's OK.

沒問題。

記憶提示

OK = all right：對，行，可以；它可非動詞、形容詞和副詞，在英語裡使用頻率很高。

舉一反三

Is your room all right?

您的房間沒什麼問題吧？

201　It doesn't work. 這東西壞了。

關鍵句

It doesn't work.

這東西壞了。

I will have it repaired.

我會把它修好的。

記憶提示

你吃了醫生給你開的藥，醫生問你這藥管不管用，如果不管用，你也可以說「It doesn't work」。

舉一反三

（1）It is broken.

這個壞了。

（2）It is spoiled.

這個壞了。

202　We'll send someone to repair it right now. 我們會馬上派人去修。

關鍵句

We'll send someone to repair it right now.

我們會馬上派人去修。

I will wait for him in the room.

我在房間裡等他。

記憶提示

repair ＝ fix：修理。

舉一反三

（1）We'll send someone to fix it right now.
我們會馬上派人去修。

（2）We'll send someone to mend it as soon as possible.
我們會馬上派人去修。

203　The water tap dripped all night long. I could hardly sleep. 水龍頭滴了一夜，我很難入睡。

關鍵句

The water tap dripped all night long. I could hardly sleep.

水龍頭滴了一夜，我很難入睡。

Sorry for that. I'm going to fix it right now.

很抱歉。我馬上過去修。

記憶提示

water tap：水龍頭，也可用 faucet。

舉一反三

The water faucet leaked the whole night. I couldn't fall asleep.

水龍頭滴了一夜，我很難入睡。

204   The toilet doesn't flush. 馬桶不能沖水。

關鍵句

The toilet doesn't flush.

馬桶不能沖水。

I'll fix it.

我會把它修好的。

記憶提示

toilet：廁所，洗手間。

關於「廁所」的說法，無論在東方還是西方都有很多種。如英國人說 loo，澳洲人說 happy house。另外還有諸如 restroom, ladies, Ladies' room, men's, men's room 等說法。

舉一反三

（1）The toilet doesn't work.
廁所壞了。

（2）The toilet is broken.
廁所壞了。

205　The bathtub is leaking. 浴缸漏水了。

關鍵句

The bathtub is leaking.

浴缸漏水了。

We'll be there to fix it in minutes.

我們馬上就過去修。

記憶提示

bathtub：浴缸；leaking：漏水。

舉一反三

The bathtub is leaky.

浴缸漏水了。

206　The air conditioner in the room is broken. 房間裡的空調壞了。

關鍵句

The air conditioner in the room is broken.

房間裡的空調壞了。

It worked very well yesterday evening.

昨天傍晚還挺好的。

記憶提示

broken 和 is 組成表語，表示「壞了」；用於汽車時，可譯成「拋錨了」。

舉一反三

The air conditioning in the room doesn't work.

房間裡的空調壞了。

---

207 The electric light in the room is out of order. 房間裡的燈壞了。

關鍵句

The electric light in the room is out of order.

房間裡的燈壞了。

Fortunately I have got an electric torch.

幸虧我有手電筒。

記憶提示

electric light：電燈；electric bulb：燈泡。

out of order 也可說 go wrong。

舉一反三

（1）The electric light in the room is out of order.

房間裡的電燈壞了。

（2）There is something wrong with the electric bulb in the room.

房間裡的電燈泡壞了。

Section V　Telephone Service 電話服務

208　This is the front desk. 這裡是櫃檯。

關鍵句

This is the front desk.

這裡是櫃檯。

Can I speak to the duty manager?

我找值班經理。

記憶提示

front desk ＝ reception：櫃檯。

舉一反三

（1）This is reception.

這裡是櫃檯。

（2）Reception, can I help you?

這裡是櫃檯，需要幫忙嗎？

209　May I speak to Mr.Wang? 請王先生接電話好嗎？

關鍵句

May I speak to Mr.Wang?

請王先生接電話好嗎？

One moment, please.

請稍等。

記憶提示

speak = talk = converse：談話。

舉一反三

May I have a word with Mr.Wang?

請王先生接電話好嗎？

210　I'll put you through. 我為您轉接過去。

關鍵句

I'll put you through.

我為您轉接過去。

Thank you.

謝謝你。

記憶提示

put through：轉接電話。電話接線員常用這個詞。

舉一反三

（1）I'll connect the extension for you.

我為您轉接到分機去。

（2）I'll put you through to the manager.

我為您轉接到經理那裡去。

211　Hold on, please. 請不要掛斷。

關鍵句

Hold on, please.

請不要掛斷。

All right.

好的。

記憶提示

hold on：不要掛斷。電話用語。

舉一反三

（1）Hang on, please.
請不要掛斷。

（2）A moment, please.
請稍候。

212　Sorry, the number is engaged. 對不起，電話占線。

關鍵句

Sorry, the number is engaged.

對不起，電話占線。

I'll call back later.

我待會再打。

記憶提示

engaged：使用的，被占用的，繁忙的；已訂婚的。

舉一反三

（1）Sorry, the number is occupied.

對不起，電話占線。

（2）Sorry, the line is busy.

對不起，電話占線。

213　I'm afraid Miss Liu is not in. 恐怕劉小姐出去了。

關鍵句

I'm afraid Miss Liu is not in.

恐怕劉小姐出去了。

Would you please tell her that Mary called?

請您告訴她瑪麗有打電話給她。

記憶提示

注意：afraid 是形容詞，意為「擔心的、害怕的」，多與助動詞 be 連用。「I'm afraid（that）...」是一個常用句型，意為「我恐怕……」。

例如：

She is afraid of dog.

她怕狗。

I'm afraid (that) you got the wrong number.

恐怕您弄錯號碼了。

舉一反三

（1）I'm afraid Miss Liu is not here at the moment.

劉小姐現在不在這裡。

（2）I'm afraid Miss Liu is out.
劉小姐出去了。

214   Would you like to leave a message? 您想留言嗎？

關鍵句

Would you like to leave a message?
您想留言嗎？
OK, I'll leave a message.
好的，我留一下言。

記憶提示

leave 在這裡是「留下」，而不是「離開」的意思。

舉一反三

Would you like to drop a message?
您願意留言嗎？

215   Can you call again later? 您能待會再打來嗎？

關鍵句

Can you call again later?
您能待會再打來嗎？
Yes, I'll call later.
好的，我待會再打來。

記憶提示

call sb. = ring sb.up：給某人打電話。

舉一反三

（1）Could you phone again later?

您能待會再打來嗎？

（2）Would you give a ring again later?

您能待會再打來嗎？

216 I'd like to make a collect call to the US. 我想撥打到美國的對方付費電話。

關鍵句

I'd like to make a collect call to the US.

我想撥打到美國的對方付費電話。

What number do you want to call?

請問電話號碼是多少？

記憶提示

collect call 指「對方付費電話」，打國際長途到一些國家可打對方付費電話。把要通話的城市和要接通的號碼告知接線員即可。

舉一反三

I want to make a collect call to the US.

我想撥打到美國的對方付費電話。

217　Would you please tell me the country code of the UK? 您能告訴我英國的國家電話代碼嗎？

關鍵句

Would you please tell me the country code of the UK?

您能告訴我英國的國家電話代碼嗎？

The country code of the UK is 44.

英國的電話區號是 44。

記憶提示

UK = United Kingdom：聯合王國，即英國。

country code：國家電話代碼。

舉一反三

What's the area code of the U.K.?

請問英國的國家電話代碼是多少？

218　Would you like a pay call or a collect call? 您想要付費 電話還是對方付款電話？

關鍵句

Would you like a pay call or a collect call?

您想要付費電話還是對方付款電話？

Pay call, please.

直接付費。

記憶提示

pay call 是「直接付費電話」，collect call 是「對方付費電話」。

舉一反三

（1）You'd rather like a pay call or a collect call?
　　您想要付費電話還是對方付款電話？

（2）What do you prefer, a pay call or a collect call?
　　您想要付費電話還是對方付款電話？

Section VI　Hotel Extension & Checking out 住宿延期及退房

219　For how many nights do you wish to extend? 您想延長幾晚？

關鍵句

For how many nights do you wish to extend?

您想延長幾晚？

I would like to extend two nights more.

我想延長兩晚。

記憶提示

extend ＝ prolong：延長。

193

（1）For how many nights do you wish to prolong?
您想延長幾晚？

（2）How many more days are you going to stay?
您想延長幾天？

220　Are you checking out now? 您要現在退房嗎？

關鍵句

Are you checking out now?

您要現在退房嗎？

Yes, I am.

是的。

記憶提示

check in：登記入住；check out：退房結帳。

舉一反三

Are you leaving the hotel now?

您要離開飯店嗎？

221　Here's your bill. 這是您的帳單。

關鍵句

Here's your bill.

這是您的帳單。

How much shall I pay?

我該付多少錢？

記憶提示

bill 可指「帳單」，也可指「鈔票」。

舉一反三

（1）Your bill is this one.

這張是您的帳單。

（2）It's your bill.

這是您的帳單。

222 The total is 1200 NT dollars. 總計 1,200 元新臺幣。

關鍵句

The total is 1,200 NT dollars.

總計 1,200 元新臺幣。

Here you are.

這些給你。

記憶提示

total ＝ in all：總共。

舉一反三

（1）300 dollars in all.

總計 300 元。

（2）Altogether it is 300 dollars.

總計 300 元。

223　Here is your change and receipt. 這是找您的零錢及收據。

關鍵句

> Here is your change and receipt.
> 這是找您的零錢及收據。
> Should I keep the receipt well?
> 我需要留著這張收據嗎？

記憶提示

> change：找的零錢；receipt：收據。

舉一反三

（1）Your change and receipt are here.
　　這是找您的錢和收據。

（2）Please take your change and receipt.
　　請拿好您的錢和收據。

224　Please make sure you don't leave any of your belongings in your room before you check out. 退房前請確認一下，不要把自己的物品遺落在房間裡。

關鍵句

> Please make sure you don't leave any of your belongings in your room before you check out.
> 退房前請確認一下，不要把自己的物品遺落在房間裡。

OK, I will.

好的，我會的。

記憶提示

make sure：確保。

leave 作名詞時指「許可、休假」，作動詞時指「離開、動身、遺棄」。

舉一反三

Please make sure whether you take all your belongings with you before you check out the hotel.

退房前請檢查一下是否帶齊了自己的物品。

225 Thank you for being with us. 謝謝光臨本店。

關鍵句

Thank you for being with us.

謝謝光臨本店。

I am very satisfied with the service at your hotel.

我對你們飯店的服務非常滿意。

記憶提示

thank you 是講英語國家的人使用頻率最高的字眼之一，這已成為習慣，這也是所謂「禮多人不怪」的道理。

be with us：和我們在一起，這裡指「光臨本店」。

舉一反三

Thank you for staying with us.

謝謝光臨本店。

Dialogue 典型對話示例

（Ⅰ）

A：There are different star-rated hotels in Taipei.

臺北有各種星級飯店。

Which hotel would you like to reserve?

您想要預訂哪家飯店？

B：I'd like to reserve the East Hotel.

我要預訂東方飯店。

A：The hotel is located in the center of Taipei.

這家飯店坐落在臺北市中心。

B：That's great.

太好了。

（Ⅱ）

A：Good morning. Do you have a reservation with us?

早安。您有預訂嗎？

B：Yes, we do.

有。

A：May I have your name, please?

請問您貴姓？

B：John Smith.

約翰·史密斯。

A：Please wait a minute. I'll check the list... Yes, here it is.

請稍等。我查一下預訂單……找到了。

Would you fill out the registration form, please?

請您填一下登記表，好嗎？

And may I take an imprint of your credit card?

我刷一下您的信用卡，好嗎？

B：Here you are.

給你。

A：Thank you. Here are your room card and breakfast coupon.

謝謝。這是您的房卡和早餐券。

Hope you enjoy your stay with us.

希望您在此住得愉快。

B：Thank you very much.

謝謝。

（Ⅲ）

A：Good afternoon. Front desk.

午安。這裡是櫃檯。

B：May I speak to Mr.Wang?

請王先生接電話好嗎？

A：I'll put you through.

我給您接過去。

Sorry, the number is engaged.

對不起，電話占線。

Would you like to leave a message?

您需要留言嗎？

B：OK, I'll leave a message.

好的，我留個話。

（Ⅳ）

A：Is your room OK?

您的房間沒什麼問題吧？

B：The water tap dripped all night long. I could hardly sleep.

水龍頭滴了一夜，我很難入睡。

A：We'll send someone to repair it right now.

我們會馬上派人去修。

Unit 5   Accommodations 住宿

Unit 6
Shopping 購物

Unit 6　Shopping 購物

重點單字

traditional	傳統的
product	產品
porcelain	瓷器
Cloisonné	景泰藍
handicraft	手工藝品
lacquer carving	漆雕
arts and crafts	工藝品
embroidery	刺繡
paper cutting	剪紙
countryside	農村
cashmere sweaters	喀什米爾羊毛衣
quality	質量
silk	絲綢
tie	領帶
be worth buying	值得買
sandal wood	檀香木
fan	扇子
smell	味道
time-honored	歷史悠久的
pharmacy	藥店
pinwheel	風車
available	可用到的
temple fair	廟會
Chinese Lunar New Year	春節

dough figurine	捏麵人
skillful work	技藝
pedestrian street	徒步區
famous	著名的
shopping center	購物中心
gift	禮物
relative	親戚
jade bracelet	玉手鐲
present	禮物
recommend	推薦
blue	藍色的
tablecloth	桌布
pretty	漂亮的
discount	折扣
price	價格
fixed	固定的
look at	看
display	陳列
guidebook	旅遊指南
bookstore	書店
size	大小，尺寸
shoe	鞋
necklace	項鏈
fit	合適的
traveler's check	旅行支票

| Section | 1 | Traditional Products 傳統特產 |

226　These are traditional Chinese handicrafts. 這些是中國的傳統工藝品。

關鍵句

These are traditional Chinese handicrafts.

這些是中國的傳統工藝品。

They are very delicate.

這些工藝品很精巧。

記憶提示

product：產品，產物。produce：產物，農產品。前者是名詞，後者可用作名詞或動詞，用作名詞時與動詞重音不一樣。

舉一反三

（1）These are traditional Chinese art and crafts.

這些是中國的傳統工藝品。

（2）These are traditional Chinese craftworks.

這些是中國的傳統工藝品。

227　Chinese porcelain enjoys a long history. 中國瓷器歷史悠久。

關鍵句

Chinese porcelain enjoys a long history.

中國瓷器歷史悠久。

Yes, it's world famous.

中國瓷器世界聞名。

記憶提示

porcelain ＝ china：瓷器。注意：china 第一個字母要小寫，區別於 China（中國）。

舉一反三

（1）Chinese porcelain has a long history.

中國瓷器歷史悠久。

（2）The history of Chinese porcelain is a long one.

中國瓷器歷史悠久。

228 Cloisonné is a traditional handicraft. 景泰藍是一種傳統工藝品。

關鍵句

Cloisonné is a traditional handicraft.

景泰藍是一種傳統工藝品。

It's also fine and durable.

它還很精美耐用。

記憶提示

cloisonné：景泰藍，源自明朝景泰年間，距今已有五百多年；它是一種用銅做坯胎，外塗礦石粉、顏料、水的混合物，經高溫燒製而成。又可稱為 enamel ware。

舉一反三

（1）Cloisonné is a kind of traditional handicraft.
景泰藍是一種傳統工藝品。

（2）Cloisonné is a kind of enamel ware.
景泰藍是一種琺瑯製品。

229　Lacquer carving is a kind of traditional art and crafts. 漆雕是一種傳統工藝。

關鍵句

Lacquer carving is a kind of traditional art and crafts.
漆雕是一種傳統工藝。

The red color of lacquer is a symbol of good luck.
漆雕的紅顏色象徵吉祥。

記憶提示

carving 是名詞，指「雕刻、雕刻品」；carve 是動詞，指「雕刻、切開」。

舉一反三

（1）Lacquer carving is one of the traditional arts and crafts.
漆雕是一種傳統工藝。

（2）Lacquer carving is a variety of traditional arts and crafts.
漆雕是一種傳統工藝。

230 Suzhou embroidery is one of the four well-know embroideries in China. 蘇繡是中國四大名繡之一。

關鍵句

Suzhou Embroidery is one of the four well-known embroi-deries in China.

蘇繡是中國四大名繡之一。

This work with cat and fish design looks good.

這幅刺有魚和貓圖案的繡品很好看。

記憶提示

embroidery＝broider：刺繡，用針和線繡出的織品。

舉一反三

（1）The Suzhou needlework of cat and fish looks good.

這幅刺有魚和貓的蘇繡很好看。

（2）The Suzhou stitchwork of cat and fish is pretty.

這幅刺有魚和貓的蘇繡很好看。

231 Paper cutting is popular in the countryside of north China. 剪紙在中國北方農村很流行。

關鍵句

Paper cutting is popular in the countryside of north China.

剪紙在中國北方農村很流行。

It is of high artistic value。

它具有很高的藝術價值。

Unit 6　Shopping 購物

記憶提示

popular ＝ trendy：流行。

countryside ＝ rural area：農村；country：國家、鄉村。

舉一反三

（1）Paper cutting is trendy in the countryside of northern China.
剪紙在中國北方農村很流行。

（2）Everybody likes paper cutting in the countryside of north China.
在中國北方農村，大家都喜歡剪紙。

232　Chinese Cashmere sweaters are of good quality.　中國的喀什米爾羊毛衣品質很好。

關鍵句

Chinese Cashmere sweaters are of good quality.
中國的喀什米爾羊毛衣品質很好。

The price is reasonable.
價格合理。

記憶提示

cashmere sweater：喀什米爾羊毛衣。

quality：質量；quantity：數量。

舉一反三

（1）The Chinese Cashmere sweaters are well made.
中國的喀什米爾羊毛衣品質很好。

（2）Chinese make high quality cashmere sweaters.

中國的喀什米爾羊毛衣品質很好。

233　The Chinese silk tie is worth buying. 中國絲綢領帶值得買。

關鍵句

The Chinese silk tie is worth buying.

中國絲綢領帶值得買。

I would like to buy one。

我想買一條。

記憶提示

worth buying：值得買，可用這種方法構成多個短語，如：值得參觀 worth visiting，值得學習 worth learning。

舉一反三

The Chinese silk tie is a good buy.

中國絲綢領帶值得買。

234　Sandal wood fans smell good. 檀香扇的味道很好聞。

關鍵句

Sandal wood fans smell good.

檀香扇的味道很好聞。

It is an ideal gift.

這是一種理想的禮物。

記憶提示

sandal wood：檀香木。

smell 作名詞時指「氣味、嗅覺」，作動詞時指「聞到、嗅」。

舉一反三

（1）Sandal wood fans smell nice.
　　　檀香扇的味道很好聞。

（2）Sandal wood fans smell fragrant.
　　　檀香扇的味道很香。

235　Tongrentang is a 300-year-old time-honored pharmacy. 同仁堂是一個有 300 年歷史的老字號藥店。

關鍵句

Tongrentang is a 300-year-old time-honored pharmacy.

同仁堂是一個有 300 年歷史的老字號藥店。

It sells nice medicine.

同仁堂銷售很好的藥。

記憶提示

time-honored ＝ time-honoured：古老而受到尊敬的。

舉一反三

（1）Tongrentang is a 300-year-old famous brand pharmacy.
　　　同仁堂是一個有 300 年歷史的老字號藥店。

（2）Tongrentang is a pharmacy with a 300-year-old history.
　　　同仁堂是一個有 300 年歷史的老字號藥店。

236 Pinwheels are available at Temple Fairs during the Chinese New Year. 春節廟會上有賣風車。

關鍵句

Pinwheels are available at Temple Fairs during the Chinese New Year.

春節廟會上有賣風車。

I would get one for my son.

我得給我兒子買個風車。

記憶提示

fair：定期集市，展銷會。因在寺廟前舉行所以叫「廟會」（temple fair）。

舉一反三

（1）Pinwheels are on offer at Temple Fairs during the Chinese New Year.

春節廟會上有賣風車。

（2）Pinwheels are on sale at Temple Fairs during the Chinese New Year.

春節廟會上有賣風車。

237 Making dough figurines is skillful work. 捏麵人是個技藝。

關鍵句

Making dough figurines is skillful work.

捏麵人是個技藝。

It must take long time to make.

肯定要花很長時間才能做好。

記憶提示

dough figurine 是捏麵人，dough 是生麵糰。

skillful work：技藝。

舉一反三

（1）Making dough figurines is delicate work.
捏麵人是個技藝。

（2）dough figurines making is skilled work.
捏麵人是個技藝。

Section II　Go Shopping 血拼

238　Dubai Mall is a world famous shopping center in Beijing. 杜拜購物中心是世界著名的購物中心。

關鍵句

Dubai Mall is a world famous shopping center in Beijing.
杜拜購物中心是世界著名的購物中心。

I would go there to shop.
我想去那裡購物。

記憶提示

pedestrian street ＝ walking street：徒步區。

舉一反三

Dubai Mall is a world famous shopping mall in Arab.

阿拉伯杜拜購物中心是世界著名的購物中心。

239 What can I do for you? 有什麼需要幫忙的嗎？

關鍵句

What can I do for you?

有什麼需要幫忙的嗎？

I would like to see the blue sweater over there.

我想看一下那邊的藍色毛衣。

記憶提示

在購物語境中，問「我能幫忙嗎」，言下之意就是「你有什麼想看（想買）的嗎」。這句話在服務行業裡用得很廣泛。

舉一反三

Can I help you?

我能幫忙嗎？

240 We'd like to buy some gifts for friends. 我們想給朋友買點禮物。

關鍵句

We'd like to buy some gifts for friends.

我們想給朋友買點禮物。

I think you can get what you want here.

我想您會在這裡買到您想要的東西的。

記憶提示

gift ＝ present：禮品。

舉一反三

We need to buy some presents for friends.

我們要給朋友買點禮物。

241　A jade bracelet is a good present. 玉手鐲是個好禮物。

關鍵句

A jade bracelet is a good present.

玉手鐲是個好禮物。

I think so.

我也覺得是。

記憶提示

jade：玉；bracelet：手鐲；jade bracelet：玉手鐲。

舉一反三

（1）A jade bracelet is a good gift.
　　　玉手鐲是個好禮物。

（2）A jade bracelet is an ideal present.
　　　玉手鐲是個好禮物。

242 Could I recommend this? 我可以給您推薦這個嗎？

關鍵句

Could I recommend this?

我可以給您推薦這個嗎？

Yes, please.

好啊。

記憶提示

recommend：推薦。

舉一反三

Would you like to have a look at this?

您看看這個好嗎？

243 How about this blue one? 這個藍色的怎麼樣？

關鍵句

How about this blue one?

這個藍色的怎麼樣？

It is quite nice.

蠻不錯的。

記憶提示

how about：……怎樣；blue：藍色的。

舉一反三

（1）Is this blue one all right?
這個藍色的可以嗎？

（2）Is the blue one OK?
這個藍色的行嗎？

244　This tablecloth looks nice. 這塊桌布很好看。

關鍵句

This tablecloth looks nice.
這塊桌布很好看。

I like it very much.
我非常喜歡。

記憶提示

tablecloth：桌布，是複合名詞；tableware：餐具。

舉一反三

（1）This tablecloth is beautiful.
這塊桌布很好看。

（2）This tablecloth looks pretty.
這塊桌布很好看。

245 Is this the one you want? 您是想要這個嗎？

關鍵句

Is this the one you want?

您是想要這個嗎？

Yes, exactly.

是的。

記憶提示

one 這裡是代詞，也可作數詞；want：想要。

舉一反三

（1）Do you want this one?

您是想要這個嗎？

（2）Is this the one you'd like to take?

您是想要這個嗎？

246 Can you remember what make it is? 您記得是什麼樣式的嗎？

關鍵句

Can you remember what make it is?

您記得是什麼樣式的嗎？

Let me see.

讓我想一下。

記憶提示

see 在這裡不表示「看」，而表示「想」。

247　We give a 20 percent discount. 可以打八折。

關鍵句

We give a 20 percent discount.
可以打八折。

That's very kind of you.
那太好了。

記憶提示

20 percent discount：降價 20%，也就是我們習慣說的「打八折」。

舉一反三

（1）We offer a 20 percent discount.
可以打八折。

（2）You can have a 20 percent discount.
您可享受八折優惠。

248　The price is fixed. 不二價。

關鍵句

The price is fixed.
不二價。

Couldn't it be flexible?
不能有點彈性嗎？

記憶提示

fixed：固定的，反義詞是 flexible。

舉一反三

（1）One price only.
不二價。

（2）No bargaining.
不二價。

249 Take a look at the ones on display, please. 請看看展示的那些。

關鍵句

Take a look at the ones on display, please.

請看看展示的那些。

All right.

好的。

記憶提示

display ＝ exhibit：展覽、陳列，可用作名詞或動詞。

舉一反三

（1）Have a look at the ones on display, please.
請看看陳列的那些。

（2）Take a look at the ones on exhibition, please.
請看看擺著的那些。

250　Is the guidebook available in the bookstore? 這本旅遊指南在書店裡還有賣嗎？

關鍵句

Is the guidebook available in the bookstore?

這本旅遊指南在書店裡還有賣嗎？

Yes, there are many of them in the bookstore.

旅遊指南在書店裡有很多。

記憶提示

bookstore 也可說成 bookshop。

舉一反三

（1）Can we get the guidebook in the bookstore?

這本旅遊指南在書店裡能買到嗎？

（2）Do they sell the guidebook in the bookstore?

這本旅遊指南在書店裡有賣的嗎？

251.　What size shoes do you want? 您要多大號的鞋？

關鍵句

What size shoes do you want?

您要多大號的鞋？

Number 28, please.

我要 28 號的。

記憶提示

size：尺碼。問鞋子、衣服、帽子等的尺碼大小都要用這個詞。

舉一反三

（1）How big do you want the shoes?
您要多大號的鞋？

（2）What size shoes would you like?
您想要多大號的鞋？

25　This necklace doesn't fit me. 這條項鏈不適合我。

關鍵句

This necklace doesn't fit me.

這條項鏈不適合我。

We have many others for you to choose from.

我們有很多其他款式可供您選擇。

記憶提示

fit ＝ suit：適合。

舉一反三

This necklace doesn't suit me.

這條項鏈不適合我。

253　Can I pay with a traveler's check? 我能用旅行支票付費嗎？

關鍵句

Can I pay with a traveler's check?

我能用旅行支票付費嗎？

Sure you can.

當然可以。

記憶提示

traveler's check：旅行支票。

舉一反三

（1）Is the traveler's check taken by your store?

你們店收旅行支票嗎？

（2）Can I use traveler's checks here?

這裡能使用旅行支票嗎？

Dialogue 典型對話示例

A：What can I do for you?

我能幫忙嗎？

B：We'd like to buy some gifts for friends.

我們想給朋友買點禮物。

A：May I recommend this?

我可以給您推薦這個嗎？

It's cloisonné, a traditional handicraft.

這是景泰藍，一種傳統工藝品。

B：It's not the one I want.

不是我想要的。

A：Take a look at the Suzhou embroidery on display, please. They are of good quality.

請看看展示的那些蘇繡，質量非常好。

We give a 20 percent discount.

可以給您打八折。

B：Can I pay with a traveler's check?

我能用旅行支票付費嗎？

A：Sure you can.

當然可以。

B：Then I'll choose one of those embroidery works.

那我就挑一件繡品吧！

Unit 6　Shopping 購物

Unit 7
Entertainment 娛樂

Unit 7　Entertainment 娛樂

重點單字

Beijing Opera = Peking Opera	京劇
existence	存在
born	誕生
basis	基礎
character	角色
main	主要的
group	組，團，群
actor	男演員
male role	男角
player	演員
perform	表演
woman's role	女角
comic role	丑角
each	各自的
pattern	圖案
brilliant	燦爛的
color	顏色
painted face	花臉
symbolic meaning	象徵含義
suggest	暗示
loyalty	忠誠
uprightness	正直
enjoyable	可享受的
evening show	晚間演出

acrobatic performance (show)	雜技
ticket	票，入場券
hard to get	很難得到
handstand	倒立
contortion	扭彎（柔體）
already	已經
in vogue	流行
Han dynasty	漢代
symphony	交響樂
orchestra	管絃樂隊
wonderful	極好的
audience	觀眾
really	真正地
a good hand	熱烈的掌聲
actress	女演員
answer	回答
curtain call	謝幕
three times	三次
deeply	深深地
touched	受感動的
stage setting	舞臺布景
can't say much	說不出什麼來
leading part	主角
cancellation fee	退票費
Greece	希臘
birthplace	誕生地

Olympics	奧林匹克運動會
One World, One Dream.	同一個世界，同一個夢想。
Olympic spirit	奧林匹克精神
competition spirit	競技精神
peace and friendship	和平與友誼
higher, faster and stronger	更高、更快、更強
green	綠色的
High-Tech	高科技的
People's Olympics	人文奧運
win	贏得
reputation	名譽
table tennis	乒乓球
national	國家的
sport	運動
martial arts	武術
competitive item	競賽項目
someday	有一天

Section I About Beijing Opera & Acrobatic Show 關於京劇和雜技

254 Beijing opera came into existence over 200 years ago. 京劇成形於 200 多年以前。

關鍵句

Beijing Opera came into existence over 200 years ago.

京劇成形於 200 多年以前。

It's a very old opera.

它是個很老的劇種了。

記憶提示

opera：歌劇；Beijing Opera：京劇，也可以說 Peking Opera。

come into existence = come into being：產生。

舉一反三

（1）Beijing Opera has a history of over 200 years.

京劇有 200 多年的歷史。

（2）Beijing Opera came into being over 200 years ago.

200 多年以前就有京劇了。

255　There are four roles in general in the Beijing Opera performance. 京劇表演中的角色大致可分為四大類。

關鍵句

There are four roles in general in the Beijing Opera performance.

京劇表演中的角色大致可分為四大類。

What are they?

分別是什麼？

記憶提示

role：角色；in general：一般，大體上，通常。

舉一反三

（1）The roles in the Beijing Opera performance can be classified into four basic categories.

京劇表演中的角色可分為四大類。

（2）Actors play four main roles in Beijing Opera performance, that is, Sheng, Dan, Jing, and Chou.

京劇演員表演四種主要角色，即生、旦、淨、丑。

256　Sheng is the common name for male roles. 「生」是對男性角色的通稱。

關鍵句

Sheng is the common name for male roles.

「生」是對男性角色的通稱。

For both old and young man?

年長的、年輕的都包括嗎？

記憶提示

male role：男性角色，男角。

舉一反三

（1）Sheng can be divided into three categories: Lao Sheng (the old), Xiao Sheng (the young), and Wu Sheng (the martial art expert).
「生」可分為三類：老生、小生和武生。

（2）The male roles are known as Sheng in Beijing Opera.
京劇裡的男角叫「生」。

257   Dan refers to the female roles. 「旦」指的是女角。

關鍵句

Dan refers to the female roles.
「旦」指的是女角。

I know Dan roles are usually played by men in the old days.
據我所知，從前旦角通常是由男演員扮演的。

記憶提示

female role：女性角色，女角。

舉一反三

（1）Dan are further classified into Qingyi (the young and middle-aged woman), Huadan (the innocent and dissolute), Wudan (girls with martial arts skills) and Laodan (senior woman), etc.
「旦」可分為青衣、花旦、武旦和老旦等。

（2）In the past, female roles were acted by the male players.
過去，女角是由男演員扮演的。

258　Jing refers to the painted face roles. 「淨」指的是「花臉」（角色）。

關鍵句

Jing refers to the painted face roles.

「淨」指的是「花臉」（角色）。

Jing roles are usually with unique appearance or characters, are they?

「淨」角通常具有獨特的外貌或個性，是吧？

記憶提示

painted face：花臉

facial painting：臉譜

舉一反三

（1）Jing are the painted face roles in Beijing Opera.
　　「淨」是京劇裡的大花臉。

（2）Facial painting is a unique make-up art of Chinese drama.
　　臉譜是中國戲劇中一種獨特的化妝藝術。

259　Chou are the clown roles marked by a dab of white on the nose. 「丑」即「丑角」，其明顯的標誌是鼻子上有一抹白。

關鍵句

Chou are the clown roles marked by a dab of white on the nose.

「丑」即「丑角」，其明顯的標誌是鼻子上有一抹白。

They are always very funny.

他們總是很滑稽。

記憶提示

clown：小丑、丑角

dab：小塊（如顏料等）。

舉一反三

（1）Another name for Chou is "three-flower face".

丑角又叫「三花臉」。

（2）People gave the name "three-flower face" to the clown roles.

人們又管「丑角」叫「三花臉」。

---

260 Each of the patterns and colors of Lianpu has a symbolic meaning in Beijing Opera. 每一種京劇臉譜的圖案和顏色都有一定的寓意。

關鍵句

Each of the patterns and colors of Lianpu has a symbolic meaning in Beijing Opera.

每一種京劇臉譜的圖案和顏色都有一定的寓意。

The colors are brilliant.

那些顏色都很鮮艷。

記憶提示

pattern：圖案

color ＝ colour：顏色

symbolic：象徵的

meaning：含義

Lianpu 即 facial painting。

舉一反三

（1）Patterns and colors of Lianpu varied with each representing a characteristic.
不同臉譜的圖案和顏色會各不相同，每種都代表一種性格。

（2）There is a symbolic meaning for each facial painting in Beijing Opera.
每個京劇臉譜都有一定的含意。

261　Red suggests loyalty, while black signifies honesty and frankness. 紅色象徵忠誠，而黑色象徵誠實與直率。

關鍵句

Red suggests loyalty，while black signifies honesty and frankness.
紅色象徵忠誠，而黑色象徵誠實與直率。

記憶提示

suggest：暗示

loyalty：忠誠

signify：表示，意味

honesty：誠實

frankness：率直，坦白

舉一反三

（1）Red symbolizes fidelity and justice.
紅色表現忠誠與正直。

（2）White stands for cattiness and cunning.
白色象徵狡猾和欺詐。

262 The most enjoyable evening show is the acrobatic performance. 雜技是晚間最受歡迎的演出。

關鍵句

The most enjoyable evening show is the acrobatic performance.
雜技是晚間最受歡迎的演出。

I'm sure it is.
一定是。

記憶提示

enjoyable：可享受的

show = public entertainment：公眾娛樂，表演

acrobatic performance：雜技表演

舉一反三

（1）The most popular evening show is acrobatic performance.
雜技是晚間最受歡迎的演出。

（2）Acrobatic show is the most pleasant evening entertainment.
雜技表演是最令人愉快的晚間娛樂活動。

263　Tickets for the acrobatic show are hard to get. 雜技票很難買到。

關鍵句

Tickets for the acrobatic show are hard to get.

雜技票很難買到。

Can you book the tickets for us?

你能幫我們訂票嗎？

記憶提示

hard：辛苦的，費力的。

舉一反三

（1）Acrobatic show tickets are difficult to get.

雜技票很難買到。

（2）It's hard to get the acrobatic performance tickets.

雜技票很難買到。

264　Handstand and contortion were already in vogue in the Han Dynasty. 倒立和柔體在漢代就已經流行。

關鍵句

Handstand and contortion were already in vogue in the Han Dynasty.

倒立和柔體在漢代就已經流行。

Were they?

是嗎？

記憶提示

handstand：手倒立

contortion：扭彎

vogue ＝ fashion：流行

dynasty：朝代

舉一反三

（1）Handstand and contortion first appeared in the Han Dynasty.
倒立和柔體在漢代就已經出現了。

（2）You can find handstand and contortion performance in the Han Dynasty.
倒立和柔體表演在漢代就已經有了。

Section II Impressions of the Performance 表演觀後感

265 The symphony orchestra in the National Concert Hall is wonderful. 國家音樂廳的交響樂棒極了。

關鍵句

The symphony orchestra in the National Concert Hall is wonderful.
國家音樂廳的交響樂棒極了。

I've heard about it.
我聽說過。

記憶提示

symphony：交響樂

orchestra：管絃樂隊

concert hall：音樂廳

舉一反三

（1）The music in the National Concert Hall is marvelous.
國家音樂廳的音樂是非凡的。

（2）It's a pity if you don't go to enjoy the symphony in the Beijing Concert Hall.
不去國家音樂廳欣賞交響樂會很遺憾的。

266　The audience really gave them a good hand. 觀眾的掌聲真熱烈。

關鍵句

The audience really gave them a good hand.
觀眾的掌聲真熱烈。

They deserved it.
他們受之無愧。

記憶提示

audience：觀眾

good hand ＝ applause：掌聲

舉一反三

（1）Everybody gave them warm applause.
大家對他們給予了熱烈的掌聲。

（2）They were warmly received by the audience.

他們受到了觀眾的熱烈歡迎。

---

267 The actors and actresses answered curtain calls three times. 男女演員謝了三次幕。

關鍵句

The actors and actresses answered curtain calls three times.

男女演員謝了三次幕。

They have done a good job.

他們演得真好。

記憶提示

actor：男演員

actress：女演員

curtain：布幕

answer curtain calls：謝幕

舉一反三

（1）They got curtain calls three times.

演員們謝了三次幕。

（2）The performers received three curtain calls.

演員們謝了三次幕。

268　I was deeply touched by the play. 我被劇情深深地打動了。

關鍵句

I was deeply touched by the play.

我被劇情深深地打動了。

Me too.

我也是。

記憶提示

deeply：深深地

touched：被感動的

舉一反三

（1）I was deeply moved by the play.
　　我被劇情深深地打動了。

（2）The play struck me very much.
　　劇情深深地打動了我。

269　How did you like the stage setting? 您覺得舞臺布景怎麼樣？

關鍵句

How did you like the stage setting?

您覺得舞臺布景怎麼樣？

It's marvelous.

太棒了。

記憶提示

stage：舞臺

setting：布置

stage setting：舞臺布景

舉一反三

（1）Did you appreciate the stage setting?
您覺得舞臺布景怎麼樣？

（2）Did the stage setting suit your taste?
您對舞臺布景滿意嗎？

270 I can't say much for the play. 我覺得這齣戲不怎麼樣。

關鍵句

I can't say much for the play.

我覺得這齣戲不怎麼樣。

What a pity!

真遺憾！

記憶提示

can't say much：沒什麼可說的，表示不滿意。

舉一反三

（1）I don't think it's a good play.
我覺得這齣戲不怎麼樣。

（2）The performers upset us.
演員讓我們很失望。

271　Who plays the leading part? 誰演主角？

關鍵句

Who plays the leading part?

誰演主角？

Who knows?

誰知道呢？

記憶提示

leading part ＝ main actor：主角。

舉一反三

（1）Who is the hero of the play?
誰是主角？

（2）Who acts the main role in the play?
誰演主角？

272　How much is the cancellation fee? 退票費多少？

關鍵句

How much is the cancellation fee?

退票費多少？

None.

沒有退票費。

記憶提示

cancellation：取消

fee：費用

舉一反三

（1）Is there any cancellation fee?
有退票費嗎？

（2）Do we have to pay cancellation fee?
我們要付退票費嗎？

Section III Sports & Olympics 體育與奧運

---

273 Greece is the birthplace of the Olympics. 希臘是奧林匹克運動會的誕生地。

關鍵句

Greece is the birthplace of the Olympics.

希臘是奧林匹克運動會的誕生地。

I've been there.

我去過那裡。

記憶提示

Greece：希臘

birthplace：出生地

Olympics = Olympic Games：奧林匹克運動會

舉一反三

（1）The Olympics was born in Greece.
奧林匹克運動會誕生在希臘。

（2）The first ancient Olympic Games was held in Greece.
第一次古代奧運會在希臘舉行。

274　One World, One Dream. 同一個世界，同一個夢想。

關鍵句

One World, One Dream.

同一個世界，同一個夢想。

Is this the slogan of the 2008 Olympics?

這是 2008 年奧運的口號嗎？

記憶提示

dream：夢想

275　The Olympic maxim is "Higher, Faster and Stronger". 奧林匹克的格言是「更高、更快、更強」。

關鍵句

The Olympic maxim is "Higher, Faster and Stronger".

奧林匹克的格言是「更高、更快、更強」。

We should know it.

大家都應該知道。

記憶提示

maxim：格言

276 The Olympic Spirit is the spirit of mutual understanding, friendship, solidarity and fair play. 奧林匹克精神是：理解、友愛、團結和公平。

關鍵句

The Olympic Spirit is the spirit of mutual understanding, friendship, solidarity and fair play.

奧林匹克精神是：理解、友愛、團結和公平。

That's what we hope for.

這是我們所期待的。

記憶提示

mutual understanding：相互理解

friendship：友誼

solidarity：團結

fair play：公平

277 Green Olympics, High-Tech Olympics and People's Olympics. 綠色奧運，科技奧運，人文奧運。

關鍵句

What are the themes of the 2008 Olympic Games?

2008 年奧運會的主題是什麼？

Green Olympics, High-Tech Olympics and People's Olympics.

綠色奧運，科技奧運，人文奧運。

舉一反三

Environment-friendly Olympics, Technology-empowered Olympics and culture-enriched Olympics.

綠色奧運，科技奧運，人文奧運。

278　The women volleyball team of USA has won reputation for their country. 美國女排為其國家贏得了榮譽。

關鍵句

The women volleyball team of USA has won reputation for their country.

美國女排為其國家贏得了榮譽。

People must be very proud of them.

人們一定會以她們為自豪。

記憶提示

volleyball：排球

reputation：名聲

舉一反三

（1）USA women volleyball team is very popular in the world.

美國女排在世界享有盛名。

（2）American are proud of their women volleyball team.

美國人以他們的女排為自豪。

279 Baseball is a national sport in USA. 棒球是美國的國球。

關鍵句

Baseball is a national sport in USA.

棒球是美國的國球。

Everybody knows it.

大家都知道。

記憶提示

table tennis ＝ ping pong：乒乓球

national：國家的

舉一反三

（1）Almost every American can play baseball.

幾乎每個美國人都會打棒球。

（2）Baseball is a very popular sport in USA.

棒球在美國是一項很受歡迎的運動。

280 China's martial arts will be a competitive item of the Olympics someday. 中國的武術總有一天會成為奧運會的競賽項目。

關鍵句

China's martial arts will be a competitive item of the Olympics someday.

中國的武術總有一天會成為奧運會的競賽項目。

You are very good at them.

你們的武術很棒。

記憶提示

martial art：武術

competitive：競爭的

item：項目

舉一反三

（1）China's martial arts will be approved by the Olympics.

中國的武術會被奧運會認可的。

（2）More and more foreigners like Chinese martial arts now-adays.

當今越來越多的外國人喜歡中國的武術了。

Dialogue 典型對話示例

（1）

A：Beijing Opera came into existence over 200 years ago and was born on the basis of Hui Opera and Han Opera.

京劇是 200 多年前在徽劇和漢劇的基礎上成形的。

B：It's a very old opera.

這是個很老的劇種了。

A：There are four roles in general in Beijing Opera performance.

京劇表演的角色大致可分為四大類。

Each of the patterns and colors on the painted face has a symbolic meaning in Beijing Opera.

每一種京劇臉譜的圖案和顏色都有一定的寓意。

B：That's very interesting.

聽起來很有趣。

A：But the most enjoyable evening show is the acrobatic performance.

雜技是晚間最受歡迎的演出。

B：Can you book the tickets for us?

你能幫我們訂票嗎？

A：They are hard to get, but I'll try my best to get them.

有點難，但我會盡力買到票的。

（Ⅱ）

A：How did you like the show?

您覺得演出怎麼樣？

B：It was wonderful.

棒極了。

The audience really gave them a good hand.

觀眾的掌聲真熱烈。

The actors and actresses answered curtain calls three times.

男女演員謝了三次幕。

I was deeply touched by the play.

我被劇情深深地打動了。

（Ⅲ）

A：Greece is the birthplace of the Olympics.

希臘是奧林匹克運動會的誕生地。

B：I've been there.

我去過那裡。

We should know that the Olympic maxim is "Higher, Faster and Stronger".

大家都應該知道，奧林匹克的格言是「更高、更快、更強」。

A：Yes. "One World, One Dream" is the slogan of the 2008 Olympics.

同一個世界，同一個夢想是 2008 年奧運會的口號。

The Olympic Spirit is the spirit of mutual understanding, friendship, solidarity and fair play.

奧林匹克精神是：理解、友愛、團結和公平。

B：That's what we hope for.

這是我們所期待的。

What are the themes of the 2008 Olympic Games?

2008 年奧運會的主題是什麼？

A：Green Olympics, High-Tech Olympics and People's Olympics.

綠色奧運，科技奧運，人文奧運。

B：That's great!

太好了！

Unit 7　Entertainment 娛樂

Unit 8
Others 其他

Unit 8　Others 其他

重點單字

umbrella	雨傘
in case	以防
just now	剛才
catch sb.	聽懂某人
say it again	再說一遍
anyone	任何一個
answer the question	回答問題
bicycle	自行車
for rent	出租
how much	多少（錢）
rent	租金
mind	介意
wait for a moment	稍等一下
let sb. know	告訴某人
as soon as possible	盡快
think about	考慮
ask	問
something	某事
a little bit	有點
under the weather	不舒服
matter	原因
see a doctor	看醫生
sore throat	喉嚨痛
convey	傳遞；告知

message	訊息
suit	合適
yourself	你自己
up to sb.	由某人來決定
sunny day	晴天
temperature	溫度
degree	度
Celsius	攝氏的
autumn	秋季
date	日期
speak	說話
slowly	慢慢地
express	表達
myself	我自己
very well	很好
in English	用英語

Section 1 ｜ Communication 交流

281. Would you please speak more slowly? 麻煩您講慢一點，好嗎？

關鍵句

Would you please speak more slowly?

麻煩您講慢一點，好嗎？

Sorry. I'll repeat.

抱歉，我再重複一遍。

記憶提示

外國人講英語口音差異很大，當你沒聽清對方說的話時，可以用此句型向客人客氣地提出你的請求。

舉一反三

（1）Could you slow down a little bit?

你講慢一點，好嗎？

（2）Pardon?

請再說一遍，好嗎？

282 I can't express myself very well in English. 我不能用英語很好地表達我自己。

關鍵句

I can't express myself very well in English.

我不能用英語很好地表達我自己。

You are doing well.

你講得不錯。

記憶提示

（1）在英語中，express oneself 意思是「表達自己的想法、感情等」。

（2）in English 表示使用英語這種語言。類似的例子有：in Japanese（用日語）、in German（用德語）、in French （用法語）、in Russian（用俄語）。

舉一反三

（1）I can just speak a little English.

我只會說一點英語。

（2）I don't speak good English.

我英語講得不好。

283 Excuse me. What did you ask me just now? 對不起，剛才您問了什麼？

關鍵句

Excuse me. What did you ask me just now?

對不起，剛才您問了什麼？

Nothing important.

也沒什麼重要的事。

記憶提示

just now：剛才

ask：提問

舉一反三

（1）It was too noisy to hear your question just now.
剛才太吵了，沒聽清楚您問的問題。

（2）Sorry, I didn't quite catch your question.
對不起，我沒聽清楚您問的問題。

284　I didn't quite catch you. Will you say it again? 我沒聽清楚，請再說一遍，好嗎？

關鍵句

I didn't quite catch you. Will you say it again?
我沒聽清楚，請再說一遍，好嗎？

All right, let me repeat it.
好吧，我再重複一遍。

記憶提示

again ＝ once more：再一次

say it again ＝ repeat：重複。不能說成 repeat again。

舉一反三

（1）Would you please repeat your question?
請重複一下你的問題。

（2）Will you say it once more?
請再說一遍。

285 Can anyone tell me the answer to the question? 有誰能告訴我這個問題的答案？

關鍵句

Can anyone tell me the answer to the question?

有誰能告訴我這個問題的答案？

Better you tell us.

還是你告訴我們吧。

記憶提示

（1）anyone＝anybody：任何人，無論誰。作為不定代詞，只能指人（單數）。Any one 是一個詞組，既可指人，又可指物，意為「任何一個人或物」。

（2）注意 answer 後面的介詞應為 to，不能用 of。

舉一反三

Who would like to answer the question?

誰願意回答這個問題？

286 Would you mind waiting a moment? 您不介意稍等一下吧？

關鍵句

Would you mind waiting a moment?

您不介意稍等一下吧？

No, of course not.

不，當然不介意。

記憶提示

（1）當請求或徵求對方同意做某事時常用這一句型。「would」在此不表示過去式，表示委婉的語氣。此句型與「Will you wait for a moment」相比，較為委婉，不會導致對方反感。

（2）注意與中文習慣不同的回答方式。如果允許對方，則意味著「不介意」，回答用 No；如果用 Yes，則表示「介意」和「拒絕」。

舉一反三

（1）Do you care waiting a moment?
　　您介意稍等一下嗎？

（2）Is that OK for you to wait a moment?
　　請稍等一下可以嗎？

287　Sorry to keep you waiting. 對不起，讓您久等了。

關鍵句

Sorry to keep you waiting.
對不起，讓您久等了。
It doesn't matter.
沒關係。

記憶提示

（1）道歉時，可簡單地說「I'm sorry」。「I do apologize」和「Please forgive me」的說法就比較嚴肅了，最好說明道歉的具體原因和應承擔的責任，並提出補救的辦法。

（2）excuse 是最普通的表示歉意的詞語，語氣較輕，常用於口語，指原諒輕微的過失或疏忽。pardon 一般表示寬恕較嚴重的過失，語氣比

excuse 強。

（3）單獨用 pardon，讀升調時，表示「我沒聽清楚，請再說一遍。」

舉一反三

（1）Sorry for keeping you waiting.
對不起，讓您久等了。

（2）Please excuse me for the waiting.
對不起，讓您久等了。

288 I'll let you know as soon as possible. 我會盡快告訴您。

關鍵句

I'll let you know as soon as possible.

我會盡快告訴您。

No hurry.

不著急。

記憶提示

as soon as：盡快

possible：可能的

舉一反三

（1）I'll tell you as soon as I can.
我盡快告訴您。

（2）I'll inform you soon after I know it.
我一有消息就馬上告訴您。

289　Can I ask you something? 我可以問個問題嗎？

關鍵句

Can I ask you something?

我可以問個問題嗎？

Go ahead, please.

請講。

記憶提示

在表示「許可」之意時，can 和 may 可互換；但在已明確「已被允許」的情況下，是用 can，不可用 may 或 could.

舉一反三

（1）May I ask you something?

我可以問個問題嗎？

（2）Would you please tell me something?

請給我講講，好嗎？

Section II ｜ Not Feeling Well 身體不適

290　I'm a little bit under the weather today. 我今天有點不舒服。

關鍵句

I'm a little bit under the weather today.

我今天有點不舒服。

What can I do for you?

需要幫忙嗎？

記憶提示

a little bit：一點點。

weather：天氣；under the weather：這裡指「不舒服」。

舉一反三

（1）I'm not feeling well today.

我今天有點不舒服。

（2）It's not my day today.

今天我有點不太對勁。

291 What's the matter? 哪裡不舒服嗎？

關鍵句

What's the matter?

哪裡不舒服嗎？

I've got something wrong with my stomach.

我肚子不舒服。

記憶提示

（1）詢問對方「怎麼了？」時，用此句型。

（2）「What's wrong with...」也是「有什麼不舒服」、「出了什麼問題」的
意思。

舉一反三

（1）What's wrong with you?

哪裡不舒服嗎？

（2）What's up?

怎麼了？

292　I need to see a doctor. 我需要去看醫生。

關鍵句

I need to see a doctor.

我需要去看醫生。

Shall I go with you?

要我陪你去嗎？

記憶提示

see a doctor：看醫生，就診

舉一反三

（1）I have to go to the hospital.

我得去醫院。

（2）Is there a clinic nearby?

附近有診所嗎？

293　I have a sore throat. 我喉嚨痛。

關鍵句

I have a sore throat.

我喉嚨痛。

Do you need some soothing pill?

要些潤喉片嗎？

記憶提示

sore：疼痛的

throat：咽喉

sore throat：喉嚨痛

「胃疼」可以說 have an upset stomach。

舉一反三

（1）My throat is very dry.

我喉嚨很乾。

（2）There is something wrong with my throat.

我喉嚨不舒服。

Section III Talking about Weather & Time
談論天氣及時間

---

294 It's a fine day. 今天天氣不錯。

關鍵句

It's a fine day.

今天天氣不錯。

Yes, it is sunny and warm today.

是的，今天陽光充足，很暖和。

記憶提示

英語中有許多與天氣有關的名詞，加上詞綴 -y 可變成形容詞，來形容天氣。如：rain → rainy（多雨的）、wind → windy（多風的）、cloud → cloudy（多雲的）、snow → snowy（多雪的）、sun → sunny（陽光充足的）。

舉一反三

(1) It's a nice day.
　　今天是晴天。

(2) The weather is fine today.
　　今天天氣很好。

295　The temperature today is 20℃. 今天氣溫是 20℃。

關鍵句

What's the temperature today?

今天的氣溫多高？

The temperature today is 20℃.

今天氣溫是 20℃。

記憶提示

℃（攝氏溫度）即 degrees Celsius，℉（華氏溫度）即 degrees Fahrenheit

take one's temperature：量某人的體溫

have/run a temperature：發燒

舉一反三

（1） It's 20℃ today.

今天氣溫是 20℃。

（2） The temperature today is about 70 °F today.

今天氣溫大約是 70 °F。

296　Please bring an umbrella with you in case it rains. 請帶把雨傘，以防下雨。

關鍵句

Please bring an umbrella with you in case it rains.

請帶把雨傘，以防下雨。

I have it in my bag.

我有帶在包包裡。

記憶提示

umbrella：雨傘

in case：以防

舉一反三

（1） In case of rain, take an umbrella.

怕會下雨，拿把雨傘吧！

（2） You'd better carry an umbrella in case it rains.

你最好帶把雨傘，以防下雨。

297　Now it's autumn. 現在是秋季。

關鍵句

Which season is it now?

現在是什麼季節？

Now it's autumn.

現在是秋季。

記憶提示

春、夏、秋、冬的英文名稱分別是：spring、summer、autumn、winter。美國人通常把秋天說成 fall。

舉一反三

It is fall now.

現在是秋季。

298　What day is today? 今天星期幾？

關鍵句

What day is today?

今天星期幾？

Today is Thursday.

今天星期四。

記憶提示

（1）星期一到星期日的英文分別為：Monday、Tuesday、Wednesday、Thursday、Friday、Saturday、Sunday。它們可分別縮寫為 Mon.、

Tue(s).、Wed.、Thu(rs).、Fri.、Sat.、Sun.。注意：在縮寫結尾字母後需加符號「.」。

(2) 通常西方人把星期日作為一週的第一天，星期六為週末最後一天。

299　What's the date today? 今天幾號？

關鍵句

What's the date today?

今天幾號？

Today is September 9th.

今天是 9 月 9 日。

記憶提示

英式英語和美式英語在表達日期時習慣有所不同。如：2007 年 3 月 29 日，英式英語的順序是「日、月、年」，即「29th March, 2007」（29/3/2007），而美式英語的順序是「月、日、年」，即「March 29th, 2007」（3/29/2007）。

舉一反三

Which date is today?

今天幾號？

300　It's 7 o'clock now. 現在 7 點整。

關鍵句

What time is it?

現在幾點了？

It's 7 o'clock now.

現在 7 點整。

記憶提示

（1）「What time is it」表示「現在幾點了」。最普通的說法是「What is the time」，回答的句型是「It is...」。

（2）英語表示時間的方法是：先說鐘點，後說分鐘，如 six forty-five （六點四十五分）。另一種表示方法是：先說分鐘，後說鐘點。分鐘數值不超過半小時的用 past 或 after 來表示；分鐘數值超過半小時的則用 to 來表示。例如：

It is ten past ten. （現在是十點十分。）

It is ten to ten. （現在是差十分十點，即九點五十分。）

飛機、火車等時刻表的讀法：

15:00 It's fifteen hundred hours. （下午三點。）

09:09 It's (o) nine o nine. （上午九點零九分。）

舉一反三

（1）The current time is 7:00 now.

現在的時間是 7 點。

（2）It's 7:00 sharp now.

現在 7 點整。

Dialogue 典型對話示例

（Ⅰ）

A：What's the matter?

怎麼了？

B：I'm a little bit under the weather today.

今天我有點不舒服。

I have a sore throat.

我喉嚨痛。

I need to see a doctor.

我要去看醫生。

A：Shall I go with you?

要我陪你去嗎？

B：You're so kind.

太謝謝你了。

（Ⅱ）

A：A fine day, isn't it?

今天天氣不錯，不是嗎？

B：Yes, it's sunny and warm today. What's the temperature today?

是的，今天晴朗且溫暖。今天的氣溫幾度？

A：About 20℃. Now it's autumn.

大概 20℃。現在是秋季。

B：What day is today? And what's the date today?

今天星期幾？今天幾號？

A：Today is Thursday, September 9th.

今天是星期四，9 月 9 日。

B：What time is it?

現在幾點了？

A：It's 7 o'clock.

7 點整。

B：Thanks a lot.

非常感謝。

A：Not at all.

不客氣。

Appendix Practical Public Signs 實用
公共標示語

01. Exit ；Fire Exit ；Emergency Door (Exit)
出口；安全出口；緊急疏散出口

02. Entrance
入口

03. Danger! Keep Out
危險！切勿靠近

04. No Entry
禁止入內

05. No Admittance
禁止入內

06. Staff Only
閒人勿入

07. No Visitors
謝絕參觀

08. Detour Ahead
前面繞行

09. Beware of Pickpockets
謹防小偷

10. Cans Go Here Please
空罐頭丟棄處

11. Caution：Men at Work
注意：正在施工

12. Caution：Wet Floor
注意：小心地滑

13. Caution：Mind the Step
    注意：小心臺階

14. Caution：Mind Your Head
    注意：當心碰頭

15. Close the Door after You
    隨手關門

16. Dead End
    此路不通

17. Danger! Electric Shock
    危險！當心觸電

18. Danger! Deep Water
    危險！深水區

19. Do Not Overtake
    禁止超車

20. Do Not Touch
    禁止觸摸

21. Do Not Disturb
    請勿打擾

22. No Littering
    不準亂丟垃圾

23. No Spitting
    不準隨地吐痰

24. Don't Trample on Grass
    勿踐踏草地

25. No Smoking
    請勿吸菸

26. Smoking Area
    吸菸區

27. No Mobile Phones
    禁用手機

28. No Swimming
    禁止游泳

29. Emergency Telephone
    報警電話

30. First Aid
    急救

31. Silence Please
    請保持肅靜

32. Flash Prohibited
    禁止使用閃光燈

33. No Photos
    不准照相

34. Hands off
    請勿動手

35. In Case of Fire, Do Not Use Elevators, Use Stairways
    起火時禁用電梯，請用樓梯

36. Ladies
    女洗手間

37. Men's
男洗手間

38. Occupied
（廁所）有人

39. Vacant
（廁所）無人

40. Line Forms Here
在此排隊

41. Luggage Claim
領取行李處

42. No Jaywalking
禁止亂穿馬路

43. No Loud Talking
禁止大聲喧嘩

44. On Sale
大特賣

45. One-way Traffic
單行車道

46. Ahead Only
限直行

47. Keep Left (Right)
靠左（右）行

48. Out of Service
暫停服務

49. Pay the Full Price for Anything Damaged
如有損壞，照價賠償

50. Please Don't Pick the Flowers
請勿攀折花木

51. Please Pay Here
請在此付款

52. Please Show Passes
請出示通行證

53. Please Take Seat According to the Ticket Number
對號入座

54. Pull/Push
拉（門）／推（門）

55. Reserved
保留席位

56. Reserved Parking Area
預留車位

57. Ticket Holders Only
憑票入場

58. This Date Only
當日有效

59. No Graffiti
禁止（在牆上）塗畫

60. No Scaling
禁止攀援

Travel, not Trouble 旅遊英語帶你去旅行：

用餐結帳 × 客房服務 × 購物血拼，見招拆招，遇到老外不再嚇到待在原地

主　　編：張玲敏

發 行 人：黃振庭

出 版 者：崧燁文化事業有限公司

發 行 者：崧燁文化事業有限公司

E-mail：sonbookservice@gmail.com

粉 絲 頁：https://www.facebook.com/
　　　　　sonbookss/

網　　址：https://sonbook.net/

地　　址：台北市中正區重慶南路一段六十一號八
　　　　　樓 815 室

Rm. 815, 8F., No.61, Sec. 1, Chongqing S. Rd.,
Zhongzheng Dist., Taipei City 100, Taiwan

電　　話：(02)2370-3310

傳　　真：(02)2388-1990

印　　刷：京峯彩色印刷有限公司（京峰數位）

律師顧問：廣華律師事務所 張珮琦律師

-版權聲明

定　　價：399 元

發行日期：2023 年 03 月第一版

◎本書以 POD 印製

國家圖書館出版品預行編目資料

Travel, not Trouble 旅遊英語帶
你去旅行：用餐結帳 × 客房服務
× 購物血拼，見招拆招，遇到老外
不再嚇到待在原地 / 張玲敏主編 . --
第一版 . -- 臺北市：崧燁文化事業
有限公司 , 2023.03
面；　公分
POD 版
ISBN 978-626-357-145-7(平裝)
1.CST: 英語 2.CST: 旅遊 3.CST: 會
話
805.188　112000710

電子書購買

臉書